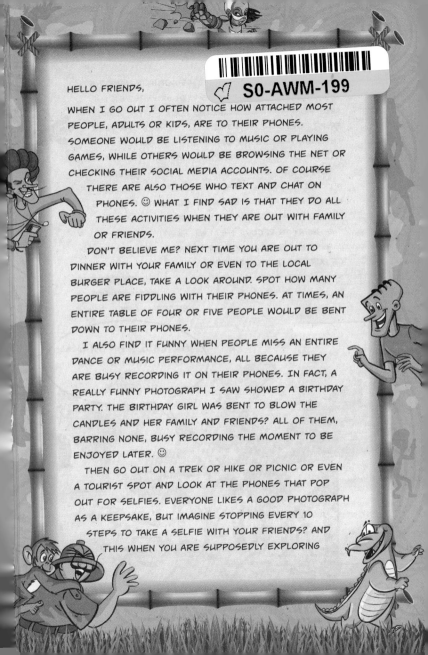

HELLO FRIENDS,

WHEN I GO OUT I OFTEN NOTICE HOW ATTACHED MOST PEOPLE, ADULTS OR KIDS, ARE TO THEIR PHONES. SOMEONE WOULD BE LISTENING TO MUSIC OR PLAYING GAMES, WHILE OTHERS WOULD BE BROWSING THE NET OR CHECKING THEIR SOCIAL MEDIA ACCOUNTS. OF COURSE THERE ARE ALSO THOSE WHO TEXT AND CHAT ON PHONES. ☺ WHAT I FIND SAD IS THAT THEY DO ALL THESE ACTIVITIES WHEN THEY ARE OUT WITH FAMILY OR FRIENDS.

DON'T BELIEVE ME? NEXT TIME YOU ARE OUT TO DINNER WITH YOUR FAMILY OR EVEN TO THE LOCAL BURGER PLACE, TAKE A LOOK AROUND. SPOT HOW MANY PEOPLE ARE FIDDLING WITH THEIR PHONES. AT TIMES, AN ENTIRE TABLE OF FOUR OR FIVE PEOPLE WOULD BE BENT DOWN TO THEIR PHONES.

I ALSO FIND IT FUNNY WHEN PEOPLE MISS AN ENTIRE DANCE OR MUSIC PERFORMANCE, ALL BECAUSE THEY ARE BUSY RECORDING IT ON THEIR PHONES. IN FACT, A REALLY FUNNY PHOTOGRAPH I SAW SHOWED A BIRTHDAY PARTY. THE BIRTHDAY GIRL WAS BENT TO BLOW THE CANDLES AND HER FAMILY AND FRIENDS? ALL OF THEM, BARRING NONE, BUSY RECORDING THE MOMENT TO BE ENJOYED LATER. ☺

THEN GO OUT ON A TREK OR HIKE OR PICNIC OR EVEN A TOURIST SPOT AND LOOK AT THE PHONES THAT POP OUT FOR SELFIES. EVERYONE LIKES A GOOD PHOTOGRAPH AS A KEEPSAKE, BUT IMAGINE STOPPING EVERY 10 STEPS TO TAKE A SELFIE WITH YOUR FRIENDS? AND THIS WHEN YOU ARE SUPPOSEDLY EXPLORING

A HISTORIC SPOT OR FOREST! THIS ACTUALLY HAPPENS WHEN I GO ON FOREST TREKS WITH FRIENDS WHO ARE PHONE-HAPPY, LEAVING THE POOR FOREST GUIDE FRUSTRATED. WHERE IS THE ENJOYMENT OF THE WALK THROUGH THE GREENS, OF LISTENING TO BIRDCALLS AND WATCHING FOR A DEER OR A MONITOR LIZARD?

HOW ABOUT JUST TAKING A DEEP BREATH AND ENJOYING ALL THAT WE HAVE ALL BEEN FAVOURED WITH—THE JOY OF NATURE AND THE LOVE OF FAMILY AND FRIENDS? I HOPE YOU DON'T MISS OUT ON ALL YOUR SPECIAL MOMENTS, IN THE HURRY TO RECORD THEM ALL. ☺

HERE IS A SPECIAL MOMENT TO ENJOY... 300 PLUS PAGES OF PURE FUN AND LAUGHTER!

HAPPY READING,
RAJANI THINDIATH
EDITOR-IN-CHIEF, *TINKLE*

AT LAST! AN ANIMAL THAT WALKS AND TALKS PROPERLY.

CLUCK CLUCK

THE HURRICANE THAT HID IN A TREE

Script:
Rina Mukherjee
Illustrations:
V.B. Halbe

ON THE OUTSKIRTS OF A JUNGLE, LIVED AN OLD WOMAN WITH HER GRANDSON, CHANDU.

CHANDU GRAZED HIS SHEEP IN THE JUNGLE. ONE DAY—

SHEEP!

I'LL GRAB ONE WHEN THE BOY IS NOT LOOKING.

SUDDENLY—

CHANDU! OH, CHANDU!

COME HOME QUICKLY! THERE'S A HURRICANE COMING THIS WAY!

A HURRICANE!

BOTH THE OLD LADY AND THE BOY SEEM TO BE TERRIFIED. HURRICANE MUST BE A DEMON!

W-WHAT IF IT CATCHES ME!

AEEII... I'D BETTER HIDE SOMEWHERE.

I KNOW! I SHALL MINGLE WITH THE SHEEP AND HIDE IN THE SHEEPFOLD.

HURRY! HURRY!

GET IN, ALL OF YOU.

THE LEOPARD ENTERED THE BARN...

...AND WAS SHUT IN.

I'M SAFE HERE.

5

6

8

THE TERRIFIED BEAR PULLED FREE...

...LOST ITS BALANCE AND FELL.

IT'S TRULY A MONSTER!

YOU WERE RIGHT, BROTHER. IT IS AN AWFUL CREATURE.

DIDN'T I TELL YOU?

ER... IT MAY BE FOLLOWING ME!

LET'S RUN!

9

WAIT!

WHO'S CHASING YOU?

WE ARE FLEEING FROM HURRICANE.

HURRICANE! AND WHAT IS THAT?

OH, IT IS SIMPLY AWFUL! A CREATURE THAT DRAGS AND PULLS ANIMALS.

I MARVEL AT YOUR COWARDICE. WE JUNGLE FOLK SHOULD NEVER BE FRIGHTENED OF ANYONE.

COME, SHOW ME THE CREATURE!

THUMP!

HURRICANE HAS JUMPED ON MY BACK!

I'D BETTER RUN.

THE SOONER I REACH MY FRIENDS, THE BETTER... AH, THERE THEY ARE.

WHY, YOU COMPLETELY MISLED ME. IT IS NO DRAGGING OR TUGGING CREATURE AS YOU'D HAVE ME BELIEVE.

IT'S A RIDER OF BEASTS! WE'D BETTER NOT STAY HERE!

AND THE THREE ANIMALS RAN AWAY AS FAST AS THEY COULD.

12

The Priest's Assistant
An Indian Folktale

Script : Gayatri M Dutt
Illustrations : Ashok Dongre

SO THE PRIEST EXPLAINED HIS PLAN TO HIS SON. THEN—

... BUT MIND YOU, UNLIKE US THESE PEOPLE ARE RICH. THERE WILL BE CHAIRS AND TABLES AT THEIR HOUSE...

... SO BE SURE NOT TO SIT ON THE FLOOR. SIT ON A CHAIR, DO YOU HEAR?

SIT ON A CHAIR... A HIGH SEAT... A SEAT THAT IS HIGHER THAN THE GROUND. DO YOU UNDERSTAND?

OH, YES, YES, CERTAINLY!

AND TALK SENSIBLY AND ON IMPORTANT MATTERS.

WHAT?

HELP ME GOD!

I SAID, TALK ON SERIOUS TOPICS ... WEIGHTY MATTERS. DOES THAT MAKE SENSE TO YOU?

WEIGHTY MATTERS? FINE, FINE! DON'T WORRY.

14

SO WITH HIS FATHER'S ADVICE IN MIND, THE YOUTH SET OFF AND SOON ARRIVED AT THE RICH MAN'S HOUSE.

HE MUST BE THE PRIEST'S ASSISTANT.

HE WAS GIVEN A WARM WELCOME—

COME, PLEASE TAKE A SEAT.

SHE'S OFFERING ME A MAT TO SIT ON, BUT FATHER SAID...

THE YOUNG PRIEST LOOKED THIS WAY AND THAT...

...AND THEN MADE STRAIGHT FOR THE COW-SHED IN THE COURTYARD.

DONE IT! AND NOW I MUST TALK ABOUT HEAVY THINGS!

KALU AND HIS WIFE, JAMNA LIVED IN THE DEEP FOREST, FAR FROM CIVILIZATION.

WE HAVE COLLECTED A LOT OF HONEY THIS SUMMER

I'LL GO TO THE TOWN TOMORROW AND SELL IT.

SO EARLY NEXT MORNING —

TAKE GOOD CARE OF YOURSELF AND GET BACK BEFORE IT GETS DARK.

KALU SOLD THE HONEY IN THE TOWN AND BOUGHT A LOT OF THINGS WITH THE MONEY.

AT ONE OF THE SHOPS —

YOU ARE A GOOD CUSTOMER KALU! HERE IS A SPECIAL GIFT FOR YOU!

OH! THANK YOU!

WHEN KALU REACHED HOME, HE GAVE JAMNA ALL THAT HE HAD BROUGHT FOR HER.

OOH! BANGLES! EAR-RINGS! HOW BEAUTIFUL THEY ARE!

KALU KEPT THE SHOPKEEPER'S SPECIAL GIFT FOR HIMSELF. WHEN HE UNWRAPPED IT—

IT IS A PICTURE OF MY FATHER!

EVERY DAY THEREAFTER—

BLESS ME, FATHER! MAY ALL GO WELL TODAY.

HE GOES TO THAT CORNER EVERY MORNING! I WONDER WHAT HE'S GOT THERE!

JAMNA DECIDED TO INVESTIGATE.

OH! NO WONDER HE HIDES IT FROM ME!

THAT EVENING WHEN KALU CAME HOME AND GOT READY TO EAT—

I HAVE NOT COOKED FOR YOU TODAY AND WILL NEVER COOK FOR YOU AGAIN!

THE FISHERMAN AND HIS DAUGHTERS

A Folktale from Kerala

Script:
Gayatri M. Dutt

Illustrations:
Ram Waeerkar

ONCE A POOR FISHERMAN DECIDED TO VISIT ONE OF HIS DAUGHTERS.

WELCOME, FATHER.

HOW ARE YOU, DEAR CHILD?

NICE PLACE YOU HAVE HERE.

I'M GLAD YOU LIKE IT, FATHER... COME, DINNER IS ALMOST READY.

THE FISHERMAN HAD A DINNER OF FISH AND TAPIOCA.

YOU ARE A GOOD COOK, MY CHILD. I MUST TELL YOUR MOTHER.

LATER—

HERE IS YOUR MAT, FATHER.

AH! NOW I SHALL SLEEP LIKE A LOG TILL MORNING.

AFTER A HAPPY STAY, THE FISHERMAN RETURNED HOME.

WIFE, WE NEED HAVE NO WORRIES. WE HAVE GIVEN OUR DAUGHTER INTO A GOOD FAMILY.

SOME DAYS AFTER THIS, THE FISHERMAN WENT TO SEE HIS YOUNGER DAUGHTER WHO WAS MARRIED TO A RICH MAN. HE REACHED THERE EARLY IN THE MORNING.

MY CHILD!

FATHER! I'M SO HAPPY TO SEE YOU!

PLEASE SIT DOWN. I'LL GET YOU WATER TO WASH.

HERE IS WATER, FATHER, AND SOME TOOTHPOWDER. YOU'LL FEEL FRESHER AFTER USING IT.

TOOTH-POWDER? WHAT'S THIS FOR?

SMELLS GOOD. I SUPPOSE IT TASTES GOOD TOO!

21

22

24

THE NEXT MORNING—

FATHER, DID YOU SLEEP WELL?

I...I....OOOH ...I DID, MY CHILD.

OH! THE MOSQUITO NET! WHAT HAPPENED TO IT?

I... I...

I'LL MEND IT QUICKLY BEFORE THE HOUSEHOLD WAKES UP.

THAT VERY MORNING, THE FISHERMAN RETURNED HOME.

WIFE, YOU CANNOT IMAGINE THE PLIGHT OF OUR YOUNGER DAUGHTER! THE FOOD AT HER HUSBAND'S HOUSE IS QUITE UNHEALTHY. IT HAS GIVEN ME A TUMMY-ACHE!

BUT WORST OF ALL WAS THE HIGH JUMP I HAD TO TAKE IN THE NIGHT. THAT WAS TOO MUCH!

I DECIDED TO RETURN HOME AT ONCE. ONE MORE NIGHT THERE, AND I'D HAVE SURELY BROKEN ALL MY BONES!

25

THE SHOW-OFF

Readers' Choice — Illustrations: Ram Waeerkar — Based on a story sent by Ajay Pahuja, Bombay

ONCE THERE WAS A RICH MAN WHO COULD NOT HELP SHOWING OFF.

THIS CUCKOO CLOCK IS FROM SWITZERLAND.

THIS IS A JAPANESE DOLL.

HOW NICE, BUT DO YOU HAVE A TALKING PARROT?

MY FRIEND HAS A TALKING PARROT.

A TALKING PARROT? I'LL GET ONE IMMEDIATELY! WAIT FOR ME...

AND OFF HE WENT TO THE MARKET-PLACE.

CAN THIS PARROT TALK?

THERE'S NO DOUBT ABOUT IT!

HERE'S A HUNDRED RUPEES FOR THIS PARROT.

!!!

27

Kalia
THE CROW

Illustrations :
RAM WAEERKAR

HOW MUCH FURTHER DO WE HAVE TO DRAG THIS LADDER?

NOT VERY FAR.

THERE'S THE TREE.

SHE HAS SEEN US.

NEVER MIND...

JUST KEEP GOING.

KEEP GOING?

BUT I THOUGHT IT WAS HER NEST WE WERE AFTER.

WE ARE... BUT KEEP GOING.

THIS IS FAR ENOUGH.

I COULDN'T ... (GASP)... GO ANY FURTHER, ANYWAY.

BROTHER ELEPHANT, COULD YOU PROP THAT LADDER UP AGAINST THIS TREE.

30

31

THE TRICK THAT FAILED

READERS' CHOICE

Based on a story sent by Ken, Kohima

Illustrations: V.B. Halbe

OH, DEAR! HERE HE COMES!

AND JUST WHEN WE WERE GETTING READY TO EAT.

COME IN, COME IN.

HELLO, MY FRIENDS. HOW ARE YOU TODAY?

IF YOU MUST.

WILL YOU SHARE OUR LUNCH?

DOES HE EVER SAY NO?

THANK YOU, I DON'T MIND IF I DO.

LATER—

HE COMES EVERY DAY, TWICE A DAY, AND ONLY FOR FOOD. WE MUST DO SOMETHING.

YES, BUT WHAT?

I HAVE IT! LISTEN...

THE SAME EVENING—

HERE HE COMES!

HOW DARE YOU SPEAK TO ME LIKE THAT!

33

THE CITY LOVER

READERS' CHOICE

Based on a story sent by Hemal Parikh
Illustrations: Ram Waeerkar

THE SUN

Script: J.D. Isloor

Illustrations: Anand Mande

YOU CAN SEE SEVERAL STARS IN THE SKY AT NIGHT...

...BUT IN THE DAYTIME, THE ONLY STAR YOU CAN SEE IS THE SUN.

IF THE SUN IS A STAR WHY DOESN'T IT LOOK LIKE OTHER STARS! WHY DOES IT LOOK LIKE A HUGE RED BALL? THE SUN LOOKS DIFFERENT FROM OTHER STARS BECAUSE IT IS MILLIONS OF TIMES CLOSER TO EARTH THAN ANY OTHER STAR. IF OUR SUN WERE AS FAR AWAY AS THE OTHER STARS, IT TOO, WOULD HAVE APPEARED TO US AS A TWINKLING SPECK IN THE SKY.

AFTER THE SUN THE NEXT CLOSEST STAR IS PROXIMA CENTAURI.

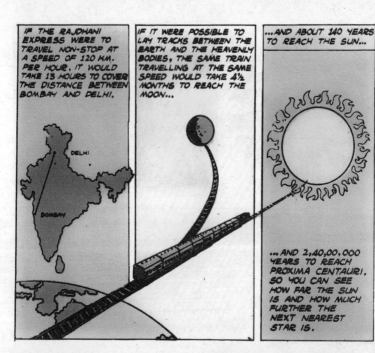

IF THE RAJDHANI EXPRESS WERE TO TRAVEL NON-STOP AT A SPEED OF 120 KM. PER HOUR, IT WOULD TAKE 13 HOURS TO COVER THE DISTANCE BETWEEN BOMBAY AND DELHI.

DELHI

BOMBAY

IF IT WERE POSSIBLE TO LAY TRACKS BETWEEN THE EARTH AND THE HEAVENLY BODIES, THE SAME TRAIN TRAVELLING AT THE SAME SPEED WOULD TAKE 4½ MONTHS TO REACH THE MOON...

...AND ABOUT 140 YEARS TO REACH THE SUN...

...AND 2,40,00,000 YEARS TO REACH PROXIMA CENTAURI. SO YOU CAN SEE HOW FAR THE SUN IS AND HOW MUCH FURTHER THE NEXT NEAREST STAR IS.

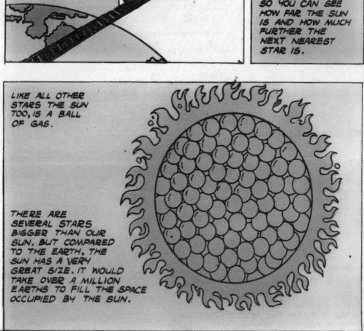

LIKE ALL OTHER STARS THE SUN TOO, IS A BALL OF GAS.

THERE ARE SEVERAL STARS BIGGER THAN OUR SUN, BUT COMPARED TO THE EARTH, THE SUN HAS A VERY GREAT SIZE. IT WOULD TAKE OVER A MILLION EARTHS TO FILL THE SPACE OCCUPIED BY THE SUN.

36

37

THE SUN-II

Script: J.D. Isloor

Illustrations: Anand Mande

IT IS VERY HOT IN MAY.

THE TEMPERATURE AT THIS TIME IS BETWEEN 35°C TO 40°C.

YOU CAN IMAGINE HOW HOT IT MUST BE WHEN THE TEMERATURE IS 6000°C. THAT IS THE TEMPERATURE ON THE OUTSIDE OF THE SUN. THE OUTSIDE IS KEPT HOT BY HEAT COMING FROM DEEP INSIDE THE SUN. THE TEMPERATURE AT THE CENTRE OF THE SUN IS 14,000,000°C.

YOU MAY NOT BELIEVE IT, BUT THAT RAY OF LIGHT COMING IN THROUGH YOUR WINDOW WAS FORMED IN THE CENTRE OF THE SUN THOUSANDS OF YEARS AGO.

IT TOOK SO LONG TO REACH THE EARTH BECAUSE IT HAD A HARD TIME COMING TO THE SURFACE OF THE SUN. IT KEPT BUMPING INTO GAS PARTICLES AND HAD TO ZIG-ZAG INSIDE THE SUN FOR CENTURIES AND CENTURIES. FINALLY IT MANAGED TO ESCAPE TO THE SURFACE AND RACED TO THE EARTH. IT TOOK ABOUT EIGHT MINUTES TO COVER THE DISTANCE BETWEEN THE SURFACE OF THE SUN AND YOUR WINDOW.

BESIDES LIGHT, THE SUN GIVES OFF SOME HARMFUL RAYS, TOO. FORTUNATELY FOR US, OUR ATMOSPHERE, WHICH IS LIKE A PROTECTIVE BLANKET COVERING THE EARTH, ABSORBS THESE DANGEROUS RAYS AND PREVENTS THEM FROM REACHING US.

THE SUN'S SURFACE IS CONTINUALLY IN MOTION AND TONGUES OF FLAME LEAP OUTWARDS. THESE TONGUES OF FLAME ARE CALLED PROMINENCES. THEY ARE REALLY VISIBLE ONLY DURING AN ECLIPSE. SOMETIMES THESE PROMINENCES REACH OUT THOUSANDS OF KILOMETRES INTO SPACE.

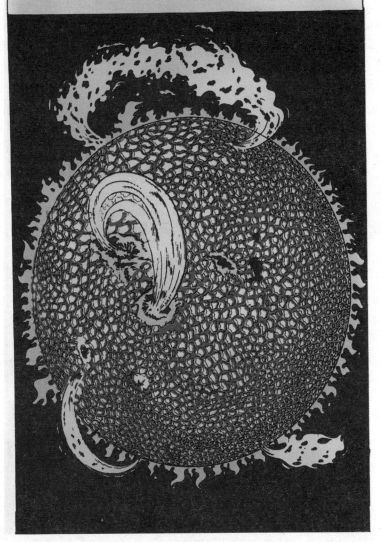

DISTURBANCES ON THE SUN CAN AFFECT THE EARTH TOO. ON 12TH NOVEMBER, 1960 THERE WAS A GREAT EXPLOSION ON THE SUN. SIX HOURS LATER A GIGANTIC CLOUD OF HYDROGEN GAS FLYING OUT FROM THE SUN, COLLIDED WITH THE EARTH AT A SPEED OF ABOUT 6400 KM. A SECOND.

FOR HOURS ALL LONG-DISTANCE RADIO COMMUNICATIONS WERE BLACKED OUT.

...COMPASS NEEDLES WENT HAYWIRE.

AEROPLANE PILOTS LOST CONTACT WITH THEIR GROUND STATIONS ...

IN SOME PARTS OF THE WORLD ELECTRIC LIGHTS FLICKERED AS IF IN A STORM. YET THE AIR AND SKY WERE CLEAR AND SILENT. SOME OF THE DISTURBANCES LASTED FOR MORE THAN A WEEK!

Prize Winning Story

This story by Ms. Sadhana Vemuganti won the Third Prize in the Tinkle Original Story Competition.

THE MAN WHO SOLD HIS MOUSTACHE

Illustrations: Ram Waeerkar

ONE EVENING, A YOUNG MAN GOT DOWN AT SITAPUR STATION.

IT WAS RAMU, THE NEW HEAD-MASTER OF THE VILLAGE SCHOOL.

RAMU WAS LOOKING FORWARD TO HIS JOB.

WHAT A LOVELY PLACE THIS IS!

ON REACHING THE SCHOOL BUILDING, HE OPENED THE DOOR OF A CLASSROOM AND—

WHAT... WHAT ON EARTH IS THIS?

HAVE I COME TO THE WRONG PLACE?

THE NEXT MORNING, RAMU MADE ENQUIRIES.

YES, RAMBABU. THE SCHOOL ROOMS HAVE BEEN USED AS COW-SHEDS FOR SEVERAL MONTHS.

AND THE CHILDREN DO THEIR LESSONS OUT OF DOORS? I'VE NEVER HEARD OF SUCH A...

...OH!

42

... WHEN—

LOOK OUT! MALLUDADA IS COMING!

IT'S MALLUDADA!

IN A TRICE, THE CHILDREN RAN OFF TO HIDE WHILE THE ADULTS FELL SILENT IN FEAR.

HMM!

SO YOU ARE MALLUDADA! WELL, YOU WILL SOON BE HEARING FROM ME.

RAMU TURNED TO ONE OF THE VILLAGE ELDERS.

SIR, MALLUDADA SEEMS VERY STRONG. BUT DOES HE HAVE ANY WEAKNESSES?

YES. ONE, HIS GREED FOR MONEY. THE OTHER, HIS MOUSTACHE!

HIS MOUSTACHE!

YES. IN FACT, WHEN IT COMES TO HIS MOUSTACHE, HE IS LIKE A CHILD WITH A PRECIOUS TOY!

LIKE A CHILD, EH? INTERESTING ... VERY INTERESTING!

IN THE FOLLOWING DAYS, AN AMUSING PIECE OF NEWS SPREAD ROUND THE VILLAGE AND REACHED THE EARS OF MALLUDADA SOON—

SO YOU ARE THE ONE WHO WANTS TO GROW A MOUSTACHE LIKE MINE, EH? ...YOU?

HA, HA, HA!

44

NO... NO! YOU NEEDN'T CUT IT OFF. IT WILL ONLY BELONG TO ME. I WILL PAY YOU RS 200 FOR IT.

WHAT?

ALL RIGHT—RS 250, THEN. I WILL EVEN OIL AND COMB IT FOR YOU TO SAVE YOU THE TROUBLE.

THIS FELLOW IS QUITE MAD! BUT RS. 250? ...UM!

THERE WAS A MOMENT OF SILENCE, THEN—

300 RUPEES IS MY PRICE!

THEN RS 300 IT IS. ANY PRICE IS WORTH IT FOR SUCH A MOUSTACHE.

RAMU QUICKLY DREW OUT A PAPER HE HAD PREPARED.

SIGN ON THAT DOTTED LINE, PLEASE.

FROM THIS DAY ON, PEHALWAN MALLUDADA'S MOUSTACHE BELONGS TO HEAD MASTER RAMU, TO HANDLE AS HE WISHES...EH?...

MALLU PAUSED FOR A MOMENT...

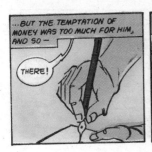

...BUT THE TEMPTATION OF MONEY WAS TOO MUCH FOR HIM, AND SO—

THERE!

EARLY THE NEXT MORNING MALLUDADA WAS WOKEN BY LOUD KNOCK.

WHO IS IT... MUMBLE... AT THIS TIME... GRUMBLE...

GOOD MORNING, MALLUDADA. IT'S ME...

...RAMU. I'VE COME TO OIL AND COMB MY MOUSTACHE.

WHY NOW? I GET UP ONLY AT 8 O'CLOCK.

45

BUT I'M IN SCHOOL BY THEN THAT'S WHY I HAVE COME NOW!

SO RAMU GOT TO WORK...

OUCH! OUCH! WHY ARE YOU PULLING SO HARD?

SO IT BEGAN, SO IT CONTINUED—THREE TIMES A DAY; EVERY DAY IN THE MORNING, DURING RAMU'S LUNCH BREAK AND AT NIGHT.

OOOOH! OUCH! GO EASY, WILL YOU, FOR HEAVEN'S SAKE?

A TIME CAME WHEN THE MOMENT HE SAW THE SLIM RAMU, THE HUGE PEHALWAN ACTUALLY BEGAN TO SHIVER.

OH, MY GOD! IT'S HIM AGAIN!

SOON, THE DASSERA FESTIVAL ARRIVED. A WRESTLING MATCH WAS HELD EVERY YEAR AT THIS TIME. MALLUDADA WAS BUSY GETTING HIMSELF INTO SHAPE FOR IT.

I'VE WON IT... HUP! ...FOR THE PAST FOUR YEARS... HUP!... AND I'LL WIN IT AGAIN.

JUST BEFORE THE MATCH, RAMU ARRIVED AS USUAL AND DID A FINE JOB ON HIS MOUSTACHE.

DOESN'T IT LOOK EXTRA FINE TODAY?

IT... OOOH!... DOES! GROAN!

THEN RAMU SMILED WIDER THAN EVER AND PULLED SOMETHING OUT OF HIS POCKET.

NOW SIT STILL, WHILE I PUT ON THE FINISHING TOUCH.

EEEK! NO! PLEASE, NOT THAT!

BUT RAMU WAS ADAMANT. HE EVEN THREATENED MALLUDADA THAT HE WOULD TAKE HIM TO THE COURT AND FINALLY, HE HAD HIS WAY!

46

WHEN MALLUDADA ARRIVED AT THE MATCH GROUNDS, THE LARGE AUDIENCE THAT HAD GATHERED AND HARI, THE WRESTLER FROM THE NEXT VILLAGE --ALL STARED AT HIM.

THEN—

HA, HA! HA!

HO, HO, HO!

HAP, HAR, HAR!

STOP IT, DO YOU HEAR ME?

BUT NOBODY WAS AFRAID OF MALLUDADA THAT EVENING ...

... HE LOOKS STRAIGHT OUT OF A CARTOON! HA, HA!

HA, HA HA!

THE MATCH BEGAN. BUT THE RIBBONS HAD BROKEN MALLUDADA'S WILL TO WIN. KNOWING THIS, HARI FOUGHT LIKE A TIGER...

...AND SOON—

CRASH!

47

HURRAH! OUR HARI WINS THE PRIZE OF RS 100. HURRAH!

THAT NIGHT, AT THE STROKE OF MIDNIGHT, RAMU CAME TO MALLUDADA'S HOUSE.

I HAVE COME TO REMOVE THE RIBBONS

RAMU'S EYES SEEMED TO BE GLITTERING STRANGELY.

I'VE ALSO BROUGHT A SPECIAL OIL TO RUB IT WITH... KEROSENE!

WHAT! OH, NO!

YOU DON'T KNOW HOW BENEFICIAL KEROSENE IS TO THE HEALTH OF A MOUSTACHE. SIT STILL!

AND RAMU MASSAGED THE MOUSTACHE VIGOROUSLY.

OOOH! OUCH!

AND NOW...!

... I'M GOING TO SET FIRE TO MY MOUSTACHE. I DON'T WANT IT ANYMORE.

...RAMU'S VOICE ROSE TO A FEARFUL SHOUT...

HELP! HELP!

...AND MALLUDADA RAN FOR HIS LIFE...

I'LL MAKE A BONFIRE OUT OF MY MOUSTACHE. COME HERE, HA, HA, HA!

NOOO... MA, MA, HE IS BURNING MY MOUSTACHE...

THE COMMOTION WOKE THE NEIGHBOURHOOD AND A CROWD SOON SURROUNDED THE TWO MEN.

RAMBABU, I BEG YOU— TAKE BACK YOUR MONEY, BUT DON'T BURN MY MOUSTACHE!

IT IS MY MOUSTACHE. I FEEL LIKE BURNING IT.

THE VILLAGERS WHOM MALLUDADA HAD TERRORISED FOR SO LONG, BEGAN TO ACTUALLY FEEL SORRY FOR HIM.

RAMBABU, I'LL BE YOUR SLAVE FOR LIFE. I'LL DO ANYTHING YOU WANT ME TO DO, BUT DON'T HUMILIATE ME ANY FURTHER.

YES, RAMBABU TAKE BACK YOUR MONEY AND LEAVE HIM ALONE.

RAMU GAZED AT MALLUDADA.

DID YOU SAY YOU WOULD DO ANYTHING I WANT YOU TO?

YES, YES...

ALL RIGHT, THEN GET YOUR COWS OUT OF THE SCHOOL.

AND CLEAN UP THE PLACE!

I'LL DO IT. I'LL DO IT.

DO IT NOW!

49

AND SO MALLU TOOK HIS COWS OUT OF THE SCHOOL BUILDING...

... AND CLEANED IT UP.

AFTERWARDS —

NOW PLEASE, PLEASE LET ME BUY MY MOUSTACHE BACK!

HERE'S YOUR MONEY I'LL NEVER TROUBLE YOU AGAIN...

OR THE VILLAGERS EITHER?

... OR THE VILLAGERS EITHER.

SOLD!

AND SO IT WAS THAT THE CHILDREN OF SITAPUR GOT BACK THE USE OF THEIR SCHOOL ...

... AND THE PEOPLE OF SITAPUR, THEIR PEACE OF MIND.

Nasruddin Hodja

WHY ARE YOU SITTING THERE, HODJA?

SOONER OR LATER SOMETHING WILL HAPPEN HERE AND A CROWD WILL GATHER.

THEN I MAY NOT BE ABLE TO GET CLOSE ENOUGH TO SEE WHAT'S HAPPENING...

...SO I AM RESERVING MY SEAT NOW!

Nasruddin Hodja

ONE DAY HODJA WENT TO SEE A MUSICIAN.

I WANT TO LEARN HOW TO PLAY THE FLUTE. WHAT ARE YOUR FEES?

THREE SILVER PIECES FOR THE FIRST MONTH; AFTER THAT, ONE SILVER PIECE A MONTH.

EXCELLENT!

I'LL START FROM THE SECOND MONTH!

Nasruddin Hodja

HODJA, WHICH IS MORE USEFUL—THE SUN OR THE MOON?

THE MOON. WE DON'T NEED THE SUN'S LIGHT DURING THE DAY...

...BUT WE CERTAINLY NEED THE MOON'S LIGHT AT NIGHT!

The Barber Meets a Tiger

Illustrations: Ashok Dongre

Based on a story sent by Sunil Deka, Nalbari

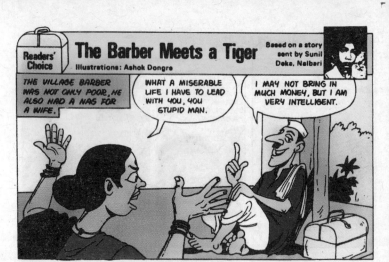

THE VILLAGE BARBER WAS NOT ONLY POOR, HE ALSO HAD A NAG FOR A WIFE.

WHAT A MISERABLE LIFE I HAVE TO LEAD WITH YOU, YOU STUPID MAN.

I MAY NOT BRING IN MUCH MONEY, BUT I AM VERY INTELLIGENT.

YOU? INTELLIGENT? POOH! OUR ONLY SON HAS NO CHAPPALS TO WEAR IN WINTER...

...WE DON'T EVEN HAVE ONE SQUARE MEAL A DAY...AND YOU CALL YOURSELF INTELLIGENT....

ARE YOU LISTENING TO ME!?

HUSH WOMAN! THIS LEAN PERIOD WILL SOON BE OVER AND OUR SON WILL HAVE A PAIR OF LEATHER SHOES AND...

...AND YOU A GOLD NECKLACE!

PROMISES — EMPTY PROMISES! I'M SICK AND TIRED OF YOUR FOOLISH UTTERINGS!

54

Again, Please!

Illustrations: Ram Waeerkar

Based on a story sent by
Kamal Borah, Kohima

TANTRI THE MANTRI

Script and Illustrations:
Ashok Dongre

ONE DAY, WHEN TANTRI THE MANTRI WAS MOVING AROUND THE CITY INCOGNITO TO SEE THE CONDITION OF THE CITIZENS, HE CAME ACROSS A PEASANTS' MEETING.

IF THE CONDITION OF THE PEASANTS IS NOT IMPROVED...

...WE MUST REVOLT!

REVOLT THEY MUST... INDEED! (HA HA)

THEY CAN DETHRONE HOOJA AND I WILL BE THE RAJA.

TOMORROW I'LL DISGUISE MYSELF AS A PEASANT LEADER...

...AND BY THE END OF THE WEEK I'LL BE WEARING THE ROBES OF THE RAJA.

NEXT DAY—

YOUR LIVING CONDITIONS ARE ABOMINABLE! YOU MUST REVOLT AGAINST HOOJA THE RAJA...

...AND GIVE A CHANCE TO THE KIND-HEARTED TANTRI TO SERVE YOU BETTER.

TANTRI WILL BE THE SAVIOUR OF THE PEASANTS.

TOMORROW WE WILL ALL MARCH TO THE PALACE... TOMORROW WILL BE THE DAY OF DECISION...

...EVEN IF I CAN'T JOIN YOU FOR SOME REASON, YOU MUST FIGHT ON YOUR OWN TILL YOU ARE VICTORIOUS.

SOON AFTERWARDS—

KNOCK KNOCK

THE RAJA WANTS TO SEE YOU, SIR.

AT YOUR SERVICE, SIR!

TANTRI, I'VE NOT BEEN WELL SINCE THIS MORNING...

...AND VAIDYARAJ HAS ADVISED ME TO TAKE COMPLETE REST FOR TWO DAYS.

SO I'M DELEGATING THE AUTHORITY AND RESPONSIBILITY TO YOU UNTIL I CAN RESUME MY DUTIES.

57

MISERLY WIT

READERS' CHOICE

Illustrations: Ram Waeerkar

Based on a story sent by Reema Kagti, Digboi

THREE FRIENDS WERE RETURNING HOME ONE EVENING.

WE MADE QUITE A LOT OF MONEY TODAY!

YES! WHAT WILL YOU DO WITH YOURS?

WELL IT IS GOD WHO HAS GIVEN US THIS MONEY.

SO, I'M GOING TO KEEP A QUARTER AND GIVE THE REST TO THE TEMPLE.

AND YOU?

I'M GOING TO KEEP HALF AND GIVE THE OTHER HALF TO THE TEMPLE.

WHAT ABOUT YOU, BROTHER?

I...ER... UH...

I'LL TIE UP ALL THE MONEY IN A PIECE OF CLOTH AND THROW IT UP...

...GOD WILL TAKE AS MUCH AS HE WANTS AND WHATEVER FALLS DOWN...

...WILL BE MINE!

DiD YOU KNOW?

The game of chess originated in India.

Originally it was a game for four players and included the use of a dice to decide moves. It had a king-piece and four other types of pieces – an elephant, a horse, a chariot and four footmen – corresponding to the four corps of the ancient Indian army. It was called "chaturanga" or "four corps".

In the 6th century A.D. traders took the game to Persia where it became known as "shatranj". From Persia it moved to North Africa and Europe.

Akbar, it is said, played the game of "living chess" with maids acting as the chess pieces, moving on the open air chequered floor of the court at Fatehpur Sikri.

Today chess is a game of skill for only two players, played on a board divided into 64 alternating black and white squares, with 32 chessmen. It is played all over the world.

Writing in Ancient India

Script: Subba Rao   Illustrations: Anand Mande

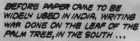

BEFORE PAPER CAME TO BE WIDELY USED IN INDIA, WRITING WAS DONE ON THE LEAF OF THE PALM TREE, IN THE SOUTH ...

...AND THE INNER BARK OF THE BIRCH TREE IN THE NORTH.

THE LEAF OR THE BARK, AS THE CASE MAY BE, WAS DRIED, SMOOTHED AND CUT INTO STRIPS.

A BOOK CONSISTED OF SEVERAL SUCH STRIPS HELD LOOSELY TOGETHER BY EITHER A SINGLE CORD PASSED THROUGH A HOLE IN THE CENTRE OR BY TWO CORDS AT EITHER END.

64

THE BOOKS HAD HARD WOODEN COVERS WHICH WERE OFTEN PAINTED.

THE INK WAS MADE FROM LAMP-BLACK OR CHARCOAL, AND APPLIED WITH A REED PEN.

SOMETIMES, THE LETTERS WERE SCRATCHED ON THE PALM-LEAF WITH A STYLUS...

...AND FINELY POWDERED LAMP BLACK OR CHARCOAL WOULD BE SPRINKLED ON THE LEAF.

LATER THE EXCESS POWDER WOULD BE BLOWN AWAY...

...AND THE LETTERS WOULD STAND OUT IN SHARP, FINE OUTLINE.

IMPORTANT DOCUMENTS WERE ENGRAVED ON COPPER PLATES.

65

THE SEVENTH IDLI.

Script: Rina Mukherji
Illustrations: Sumitra S. Sawant

VISHNUDUTT WAS VERY HUNGRY.

AH, THERE'S A MAN SELLING IDLIS!

HOW MUCH FOR THE IDLIS?

EIGHT FOR A RUPEE.

HERE'S A RUPEE.

AND HERE ARE YOUR IDLIS.

THEY'RE SO FLUFFY AND DELICIOUS

HERE GOES THE SEVENTH ONE!

OH, NO!

66

67

THE NEEM TREE AND THE GRINDSTONE

A Folktale from Karnataka

Script: Prasad Iyer B.
Illustrations: V.B. Halbe

ONCE UPON A TIME THERE LIVED A POOR BUT GENEROUS MAN. HE LOVED TREES. BUT HE LOVED THE NEEM TREE THAT STOOD NEAR HIS HOUSE MORE THAN ANY OTHER.

ALL THE SAME, HE WAS DEEPLY WORRIED.

THERE ARE MANY THIEVES IN THESE PARTS. WHAT IF THEY SHOULD CUT DOWN THIS TREE AND CART THE WOOD AWAY?

OH, NO! THAT WOULD BE TERRIBLE. I WOULD NOT BE ABLE TO BEAR THE LOSS.

AH! I'VE GOT IT!

SO HE WENT INTO HIS SHACK...

... BROUGHT OUT HIS OLD GRINDSTONE...

... PLACED IT UNDER THE TREE...

... AND SMEARED IT WITH TURMERIC AND VERMILION.

THERE! THE PLACE LOOKS LIKE A LITTLE SHRINE. NOW NO ONE WILL DARE TO CUT DOWN MY PRECIOUS TREE!

FEELING THAT HE HAD DONE A GOOD DAY'S WORK, HE WENT TO BED.

THE NEXT DAY —

LOOK! THERE'S A LITTLE SHRINE.

LET'S PRAY TO IT.

I'LL OFFER MY COCONUT.

I'VE GOT SOME FLOWERS.

AND SO —

SOON THE LITTLE GRINDSTONE BECAME FAMOUS AND PEOPLE FROM ALL OVER CAME TO PRAY BEFORE IT.

THIS MADE THE TREE VERY JEALOUS INDEED —

GRR...ALL THOSE PEOPLE MOLLYCODDLING THAT STONE! WHY, IF IT WEREN'T FOR ME, HE'D BE GRINDING HIS LIFE AWAY SOMEWHERE!

AND HIS INJURED PRIDE WASN'T HELPED ANY BY THE STONE'S SMIRKS AND BOASTS.

HO, THERE! JUST LOOK AT ME! ALL THE PEOPLE CRINGE BEFORE ME. SURELY I MUST BE THE HANDSOMEST STONE IN ALL THESE PARTS.

LISTEN, YOU LITTLE PIPSQUEAK. IF AT ALL PEOPLE COME NEAR YOU, IT'S BECAUSE OF THE SHADE CAST BY MY SPREADING BRANCHES.

AS IF ANYONE WOULD LOOK AT A DUFFER LIKE YOU!

I'M A DUFFER, AM I? WHY, YOU BIG OAF, IF IT WEREN'T FOR MY PROTECTION, THE POACHERS WOULD HAVE CUT YOU DOWN MONTHS AGO.

69

70

MEANWHILE, THE GRINDSTONE ROLLED ON AND ON—

TILL FINALLY—

I HEARD YOU CALLING (PUFF). I'VE COME... (PUFF).

OH, I'M SO GLAD. TAKE YOUR PLACE FAST. THERE COME THE TWO MEN WHO WANT TO CHOP ME DOWN.

HEY! WE CAN'T CUT DOWN THIS TREE. IT'S PART OF A SHRINE.

SO IT IS. WE'LL HAVE TO FIND SOME OTHER TREE THAT ISN'T SO HOLY.

THEY'RE GONE! WHEW! WHAT A RELIEF!

LOOK! THERE COME SOME OTHER PEOPLE.

THE LITTLE STONE. IT'S BACK. LET'S PRAY HERE.

YES, LET'S DO THAT. THE OTHER SHRINE IS TOO FAR AWAY.

A GOOD IDEA!

AND SOON EVERYTHING WAS AS USUAL. THE TREE AND THE STONE HAD LEARNED THEIR LESSONS AND REMAINED THE BEST OF FRIENDS EVER AFTER.

72

THE FOOLISH BARON

Script: Vaijayanti Wagle

Illustrations: Ram Waeerkar

THE SHEPHERD HANS LIVED WITH HIS PARENTS IN THE VILLAGE OF SNITZBURG.

THE LAND WAS RULED BY A MEAN AND CRUEL BARON.

COME ON, YOU LAZY OAF, GET TO WORK AT ONCE.

OH, THE POOR MAN. I WISH I COULD TEACH THE BARON A LESSON.

ONE DAY—

OH...OH... HERE COMES THE BARON. WHAT DOES HE WANT?

HEY THERE, LAD! WHAT IS THAT PEASANT UP TO?

WHY, SIRE, THAT IS MY FATHER AND HE IS TURNING THE EARTH'S COAT INSIDE OUT, FOR IT IS BADLY WORN OUT.

HUH...WHAT DOES THAT MEAN?

JUST THAT MY FATHER IS PLOUGHING THE FIELD. IF HE DOES NOT, THE FOOLISH BARON WILL NOT GET A PENNY.

WHAT! DO YOU KNOW WHO I AM?

INDEED I DO, MY LORD.

AND YOU DARE TO SPEAK TO ME IN SUCH A MANNER? I'LL GIVE YOU ANOTHER CHANCE. WHAT IS YOUR MOTHER DOING?

SHE IS BAKING BREAD THAT HAS ALREADY BEEN EATEN.

HUH! HOW CAN THAT BE?

YOU SEE MY MOTHER BORROWED SOME BREAD FROM THE NEIGHBOURS. NOW SHE IS BAKING BREAD IN ORDER TO RETURN WHAT SHE OWES.

BUT NO SOONER HAS SHE DONE THAT THAN SHE WILL HAVE TO BORROW AGAIN. THAT IS HOW POOR THE BARON KEEPS US.

WHY, THE CHEEK OF THE LAD. I SHOULD WHIP HIM FOR HIS INSOLENCE.

BUT WAIT, I'LL TEACH HIM A LESSON.

LOOK, LAD. COME TO MY HOUSE I WILL REWARD YOU FOR YOUR CLEVER ANSWERS.

HANS TOLD HIS MOTHER OF THE ENCOUNTER WITH THE BARON.

OH, HANS, HOW COULD YOU TALK LIKE THAT TO THE BARON! NOW HE WILL SURELY PUNISH US.

DON'T WORRY, MOTHER. IT IS TIME SOMEONE TAUGHT HIM A LESSON.

THE NEXT MORNING HANS ARRIVED EARLY AT THE BARON'S HOUSE.

HUH! YOU ARE EARLY. FOLLOW THE SERVANT FOR YOUR TREAT.

AS HANS FOLLOWED THE SERVANT OUT OF THE ROOM...

JUST AS I THOUGHT. THE SERVANT IS CARRYING A WHIP. I CAN IMAGINE THE TREAT THAT AWAITS ME.

THE SERVANT LED HANS INTO A DARK CELLAR.

WELL, LAD, THE BARON HAS ASKED ME TO GIVE YOU A SIP OF HIS FINEST WINE.

INDEED, AND WHEN I LEAN OVER TO DRINK, THE SERVANT WILL WHIP ME. I MUST THINK OF SOMETHING.

OH! BUT, MISTER. I DON'T KNOW HOW TO DRINK OUT OF A CASK LIKE THAT.

WHY, IT'S EASY.

SEE, YOU BEND LIKE THIS, REMOVE THE CORK AND DRINK. COME, I'LL LEAVE THE CORK OUT.

THIS IS MY CHANCE.

HANS SNATCHED THE WHIP FROM THE WAITING SERVANT...

...AND BEGAN WHIPPING HIM.

AH... OH, HELP! I CANNOT EVEN REMOVE MY FINGER FROM THE CASK. IF THE WINE FLOWS OUT, MY MASTER WILL BE ANGRY.

AHGGA... HELP! OW... OH!

THAT WAS A FINE TREAT. AND BY THE WAY TELL YOUR MASTER I'VE TAKEN A LEG OF MUTTON FOR MY PARENTS.

75

THE BARON WAS EAGERLY WAITING FOR HANS.

HEH! HEH! HE'S DOUBLED UP IN PAIN. SERVES HIM RIGHT.

WELL... WELL... AND HOW WAS YOUR TREAT?

WONDERFUL... JUST WONDERFUL!

AH! OW! AH!

EH? THAT SOUNDS LIKE MY SERVANT IN PAIN! LOOKS LIKE THE BOY HAS TRICKED ME.

WHEN HANS RETURNED HOME HE TOLD HIS MOTHER ALL THAT HAD HAPPENED.

OH, HANS, YOU SHOULDN'T HAVE DONE THAT.

DON'T WORRY, MOTHER. I'M GOING TO MAKE A FOOL OF THE BARON.

THE NEXT MORNING HANS SET OUT TO THE FIELDS CARRYING A LARGE POT OF PORRIDGE FOR HIS FATHER.

JUST THEN HE SAW THE BARON COME RIDING TOWARDS HIM.

AH! I HAVE AN IDEA.

HANS PUT THE POT OF PORRIDGE ON A TREE STUMP...

...AND RUSHED DOWN TO A BLACKSMITH NEAR BY TO SNATCH A PIECE OF RED-HOT IRON.

HE DROPPED THE RED-HOT IRON INTO THE POT OF PORRIDGE...

HISS

...AND IMMEDIATELY THE PORRIDGE BECAME HOT AND BEGAN TO BOIL.

NOW I'LL RUN ROUND THE POT. THE BARON IS SURE TO ASK ME WHAT I'M DOING...

HUH! WHAT ARE YOU DOING?

WHY, MY LORD. I'M COOKING PORRIDGE.

COOKING PORRIDGE! WITHOUT A FIRE? THAT'S IMPOSSIBLE.

AH! BUT THIS IS A SPECIAL POT. YOU CAN SEE FOR YOURSELF, SIRE. ALL YOU HAVE TO DO IS PUT THE POT ON A TREE STUMP AND RUN AROUND IT. THE PORRIDGE WILL COOK BY ITSELF.

THE BOY IS CLEVERER THAN I THOUGHT.

YOU MUST SELL ME YOUR POT.

OH! BUT, SIRE, IT'S PRICELESS.

WHY, I'LL GIVE YOU ANYTHING YOU WANT.

77

EVEN YOUR HORSE AND A BAG OF GOLD COINS?

HEE HEE! THAT'S A CHEAP PRICE TO PAY FOR SUCH A HANDSOME POT. THE BOY IS A FOOL.

OF COURSE, OF COURSE. HERE, YOU CAN HAVE THE HORSE AND THE GOLD.

THANK YOU.

HA HA HA! THE TRICK WORKED. THE BARON IS FOOLISH INDEED. BUT NOW WITH THIS MONEY I CAN LOOK AFTER MY PARENTS COMFORTABLY!

BUT NO ONE WAS MORE PLEASED THAN THE BARON.

HO! HO! HO! WITH THIS POT I'LL EARN FAME AND FORTUNE.

PEOPLE FROM ALL OVER WILL COME TO SEE ME AND MY MIRACLE-POT. I'LL BE A GREAT MAN.

THE BARON INVITED ALL THE PEOPLE TO COME AND SEE HIS MIRACLE-POT.

A POT THAT CAN MAKE PORRIDGE WITHOUT A FIRE!

THERE IS THE BARON'S SERVANT RUNNING AROUND THE POT TO MAKE THE PORRIDGE BOIL. WATCH IT NOW.

THAT'S INCREDIBLE!

BUT MINUTES TICKED INTO HOURS AND YET THERE WAS NO SIGN OF THE PORRIDGE BOILING.

WHAT'S THE MATTER? PERHAPS THE POT NEEDS YET ANOTHER MAN TO RUN AROUND IT.

79

CHANA and MOONG

Script: Gayatri M. Dutt
Illustrations: Goutam Sen

ONCE BRINJAL AND ONION HAD A QUARREL.

I AM GREATER THAN YOU!

NO, I AM GREATER THAN YOU.

CHANA* AND MOONG+ ALSO JOINED IN THE ARGUMENT.

I THINK MR. BRINJAL IS GREATER.

AND I AM ON MR. ONION'S SIDE.

I AM STRONGER. MR. BRINJAL IS STRONGER.

I AM GREATER. MR. ONION IS GREATER.

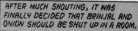

AFTER MUCH SHOUTING, IT WAS FINALLY DECIDED THAT BRINJAL AND ONION SHOULD BE SHUT UP IN A ROOM.

NOW, REMEMBER, WE'LL OPEN THE DOOR AFTER SEVEN DAYS. THEN WE'LL SEE WHO WILL PROVE TO BE THE STRONGER ONE.

SO THE DOOR WAS SHUT AND LOCKED. AND CHANA AND MOONG SAT OUTSIDE, WAITING.

ON THE SEVENTH DAY, WHEN THEY OPENED THE DOOR—

LOOK! MR. BRINJAL HAS SHRIVELLED UP!

BUT MR. ONION IS STILL IN GOOD SHAPE.

JUST THEN IT BEGAN TO RAIN AND CHANA AND MOONG WERE BOTH COMPLETELY DRENCHED.

CHANA, THE LOSER, SAT SULKING AND POUTING, HIS CHEEKS PUFFED UP...

... WHILE MOONG THE WINNER SMILED A NICE, TOOTHY SMILE...

...JUST AS SOAKED CHANA AND MOONG DO TO THIS DAY!

TIT FOR TAT

Illustrations: Hiranya Kumar Barman

Readers' Choice

Based on a story sent by Sanjay Pai

81

SEARCHING FOR SUNKEN TREASURE

Script: Padmini Rao Banerjee

Illustrations: Pradeep Sathe

OVER THE CENTURIES, MANY SHIPS HAVE SET SAIL FOR OTHER LANDS CARRYING GOLD, SILVER AND PRECIOUS GEMS, ALONG THE OLD TRADE ROUTES.

SOME OF THESE SHIPS NEVER REACHED THEIR DESTINATIONS.

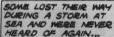

SOME LOST THEIR WAY DURING A STORM AT SEA AND WERE NEVER HEARD OF AGAIN...

...OTHERS RAN AGROUND ON REEFS IN THE MIDDLE OF THE SEA...

...AND SANK TO THE BOTTOM.

AS THE WRECKS SETTLED, THE TREASURE THEY HELD SCATTERED ALL OVER THE SEA-FLOOR.

WHAT A TREASURE LIES HERE — A FORTUNE READY TO BE PICKED UP BY ANYONE WHO TRIES HARD ENOUGH...

DIVING FOR TREASURE IS AN OLD, OLD SKILL. IN OLDEN DAYS WHENEVER A CARGO OF TREASURE WAS LOST AT A KNOWN SPOT, MEN DIVED IN TO RECOVER IT BEFORE IT SANK OUT OF REACH.

BUT MUCH OF THE WORLD'S TREASURE STILL LIES UNDISCOVERED. THE SEA IS VAST AND DEEP. AS WE GO DEEPER, THE PRESSURE OF THE WATER UPON OUR BODIES INCREASES.

DIVING EQUIPMENT HAS IMPROVED A GREAT DEAL OVER THE CENTURIES.

BEYOND A POINT, THE PRESSURE CAN EVEN CRUSH A MAN TO DEATH.

HERE IS A MODERN-DAY TREASURE-HUNTER SEARCHING NEAR AN OLD WRECK.

AH! HE HAS FOUND SOMETHING!

...FLATTISH BLACK DISCS! THEY ARE CURRENCY COINS OF SILVER, NOW DISCOLOURED.

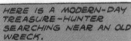

THEY ARE ALL STUCK TOGETHER, AS IF IN A LUMP.

THE TREASURE IS HAULED UP WITH A ROPE.

83

SOMETIMES A CARGO OF TREASURE MAY BE SO HEAVY THAT AN INFLATED GIANT BALLOON HAS TO BE USED TO LIFT IT TO THE SURFACE.

THE COINS AND OTHER THINGS WHICH HAVE BEEN BROUGHT UP ARE STUDIED BY EXPERTS.

WITH THE HELP OF OLD RECORDS THEY TRY TO FIND OUT WHICH SHIP HAD BEEN CARRYING THE ARTICLES, ON WHICH DATE SHE HAD SAILED AND WHAT CARGO SHE WAS CARRYING.

IF THE SHIP HAD BEEN CARRYING VALUABLE CARGO, THE TREASURE HUNTERS CAN GO BACK TO THE SPOT AND LOOK FOR IT.

SUNKEN TREASURE WAS FOUND IN THE INDIAN OCEAN OFF THE SOUTHERN COAST OF SRI LANKA ON 22ND MARCH 1961 BY A TEAM OF NATURALISTS. THE TREASURE INCLUDED MOGHUL RUPEES MADE IN SURAT IN 1702 IN THE REIGN OF AURANGZEB (1658 - 1707).

WHEN DIVERS COME UP TOO FAST !

WE BREATHE AIR WHICH IS A MIXTURE OF OXYGEN AND NITROGEN GAS. WHEN THE DIVER REACHES A DEPTH OF ABOUT 30 METRES, HE STARTS BREATHING IN MORE AIR THAN HE WOULD DO ON THE SURFACE. THE EXTRA NITROGEN HE TAKES IN GETS DISSOLVED IN THE BLOOD.

LATER, WHEN HE STARTS COMING UP, THE NITROGEN BEGINS TO LEAVE THE BLOOD. BUT IF THE DIVER COMES UP TOO FAST THE NITROGEN FORMS BUBBLES IN THE BLOOD.

THIS CAUSES ACUTE PAIN CALLED 'THE BENDS'.

THE ONLY CURE IS TO PUT THE DIVER INTO A DECOMPRESSION CHAMBER.

NITROGEN BUBBLES FORMING IN THE LUNGS

BETTER BARGAIN

A Suppandi Tale

Readers' Choice

Based on a story sent by:
Master Chingkheisel

Illustrations:
Sanjiv Waeerkar

SUPPANDI'S NEW MASTER OWNED A HEALTHY COW.

SUPPANDI, TAKE THE COW OUT TO GRAZE AND BE CAREFUL NOT TO LET IT STRAY.

WHAT A DUMB ANIMAL! IT MAKES NO SOUND AT ALL.

NOW THERE'S A TALKATIVE ANIMAL.

GRUNT!

HEE-HAW! HEE-HAW!

HEY, FELLOW! WILL YOU TRADE THIS COW FOR YOUR DONKEY?

THIS MAN IS CRAZY.

OF COURSE!

AN HOUR LATER—

GROAN! THIS LAZY DONKEY STOPS EVERY TWO STEPS.

HEE-HAW!

86

87

Shikari Shambu

Script :
Luis M Fernandes

Illustrations:
V.B. Halbe

88

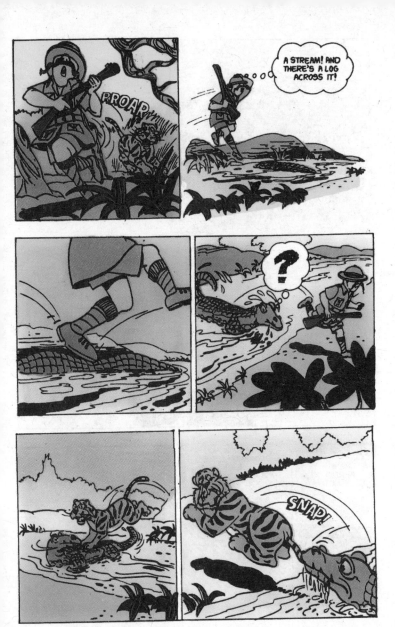

89

THE TIGER!

HE'S AFRAID OF ME!

COME BACK, YOU COWARD! COME BACK!

!

SHAMBU IS CHASING A TIGER!

HE'S FEARLESS, THAT MAN!

A Snoring Adventure

This story by Dr. Ira Saxena won the 1st prize in the Tinkle original story competition.

Illustrations: Ashok Dongre

Prize winning story

92

93

94

96

THE BOYS KEPT MAMAJI IN HIS ROOM...

...AND RUSHED BACK TO THEIR BEDS.

WHAT AN ADVENTURE!

THAT TOO, SO EARLY IN THE MORNING...

SOON, BOTH BOYS WERE ASLEEP, BUT NOT FOR LONG—

GET UP LAZY BONES!

...WHAT A LOVELY, QUIET NIGHT IT HAS BEEN!

GAURAV AND SANJU LOOKED AT EACH OTHER...

...AND THEN—

HEY WHAT'S THIS?!

THE BOYS GAVE THEIR MAMAJI A BIG HUG!

THE EMPLOYER WHO DIDN'T WANT TO PAY

Story by:
Indu Agarwal

Illustrations:
Ram Waeerkar

ONE DAY, MANY YEARS AGO, TWO MEN CAME TO SEE A RICH LANDLORD.

I AM DHARAMCHAND AND THIS IS MY BROTHER KARAMCHAND! WE NEED WORK.

YOU HAVE COME TO THE RIGHT PLACE. I WILL PAY YOU THREE SILVER PIECES EACH AT THE END OF THE YEAR...

...BUT YOU MUST DO EVERY TASK I SET YOU.

IF YOU FAIL TO DO ANY TASK, YOU'LL GET ONE SILVER PIECE LESS IN EACH OF YOUR WAGES.

THE BROTHERS WORKED HARD FROM MORNING TILL NIGHT.

103

104

105

106

DID YOU KNOW?

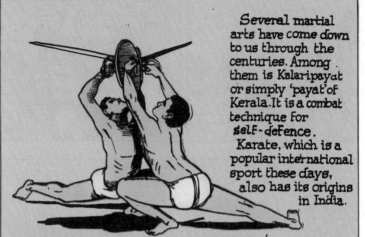

Several martial arts have come down to us through the centuries. Among them is Kalaripayat or simply 'payat' of Kerala. It is a combat technique for self-defence.

Karate, which is a popular international sport these days, also has its origins in India.

In the 5th century A.D., a Buddhist monk from India named Bodhidharma went to China to teach at a monastery there. To his dismay, he found that the student-monks were timid and weak. In order to improve them physically, Bodhidharma taught them pranayam (breathing exercises) and martial arts. These exercises became very popular in China and gradually Kempo, the Chinese form of Karate, developed. From China, it spread to Japan where it has developed to its present form. All technical terms of Karate are in Japanese. Anyone who practises Karate is called a Karateka.

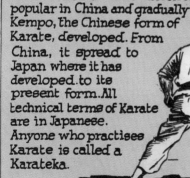

Nas'ruddin Hodja

Illustrations : Ram Waeerkar

Readers' Choice

Based on a story sent by Parag M. Potdar, Belgaum

WHERE ARE YOU COMING FROM, BROTHER?

FROM THE MOSQUE.

YOU'RE A GOOD MAN.

WHY, THANK YOU!

SO, DO YOU BELIEVE THAT ALL MEN ARE BROTHERS?

OH, YES INDEED!

AS I AM YOUR BROTHER, I HAVE A SHARE IN YOUR PROPERTY. I WANT MY SHARE.

CERTAINLY, BROTHER.

HERE! THAT'S YOUR SHARE.

WHAT! JUST ONE COPPER COIN?

I HAVE MILLIONS OF BROTHERS ALL OVER THE WORLD, SO WHAT SHARE CAN EACH ONE HAVE BUT ONE COPPER COIN?

108

A HELPING HAND

Illustrations : Ram Waeerkar

READERS' CHOICE

Based on a story sent by C. Venkatesh, Hyderabad

ORIGAMI–Hen — Mrs. Indu Tilak and Mrs. Gita Kantawala

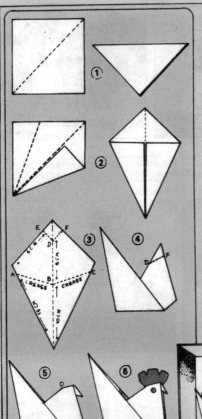

1. Take a 15 cm. square of yellow ochre paper and fold it into half.

2. Open out the paper and fold in the two side flaps as shown.

3. Turn it over and make deep creases, (AB) and (BC); and (DE) and (DF).

4. Fold up at (AB) and (BC)

5. Fold in the paper at DE and DF to make the beak.

6. Make cut-outs for eyes and comb of hen and stick them on.

Make 3-4 hens of different sizes so that you have a family. Take an old box, put some dry grass and ping-pong balls (to represent eggs) in, and you'll have a toy barn to show your friends.

KISHAN AND BISHAN

Illustrations : Ashok Dongre

Readers' Choice

Based on a story sent by Vivek Prakash, Katmandu

* BROTHER-IN-LAW

116

THE ANCIENT INSECT IN YOUR KITCHEN

Script : Ashvin Illustrations : Ajit Vasaikar

COCKROACHES ARE AN ANCIENT GROUP OF INSECTS. THEY WERE THERE TO GREET THE ARRIVAL OF THE DINOSAURS 170 MILLION YEARS AGO.

THEY WERE THERE TO BID THEM GOODBYE A HUNDRED MILLION YEARS LATER...

...AND THEY WERE THERE TO WELCOME MAN WHEN HE MADE HIS APPEARANCE ON EARTH.

AND THEY WILL PROBABLY BE HERE LONG AFTER MAN HAS GONE.

ONE OF THE REASONS, COCKROACHES HAVE SURVIVED SO LONG ON EARTH IS THAT THEY ARE NOT FUSSY ABOUT FOOD. IN HOUSES, THEY'LL EAT EVEN SUCH THINGS AS BOOK-BINDINGS, PAINT AND SOAP.

IN TIMES OF SCARCITY THEY CAN LIVE FOR ABOUT A MONTH WITHOUT FOOD OR WATER. AND TWO MONTHS ON WATER ALONE.

THEIR HORRIBLE SMELL DISCOURAGES ANIMALS FROM EATING THEM.

117

BUT THEIR BAD SMELL IS DUE TO SCENT GLANDS AND NOT BECAUSE THEY'RE DIRTY. IN FACT THEY'RE SELDOM DIRTY. THE COCKROACH SPENDS HOURS CLEANING FEET, LEGS AND ANTENNAE.

ITS ANTENNAE HELP IT FEEL ITS WAY IN THE DARK. AND IT IS WITH THE ANTENNAE THAT IT DETECTS FOOD AND WATER.

WHEN YOU SEE IT FLYING, THE COCKROACH IS USING ITS THIN FLIGHT WINGS.

Wing cover

flight wing

THE FLIGHT WINGS ARE NORMALLY COVERED BY THE HARD WING COVERS.

WE HAVE ONLY TWO EYES BUT THE COCKROACH HAS TWO COMPOUND EYES AND THREE SIMPLE EYES ON TOP OF ITS HEAD.

THE SIMPLE EYES DO LITTLE MORE THAN LET THE INSECT KNOW THE DIFFERENCE BETWEEN LIGHT AND DARK.

THE COMPOUND EYES ARE MADE UP OF THOUSANDS OF TINY LENSES. THE COCKROACH SEES A PICTURE MADE UP OF LOTS OF SEPARATE DOTS.

Compound eyes

An enlarged cut-away diagram of a compound eye

Lens

A flower as a cockroach would see it.

THE FEMALE COCKROACH LAYS 16 EGGS ENCLOSED IN A PURSE-SHAPED CAPSULE.

THE EGGS HATCH IN 2-3 MONTHS. THE SAC SPLITS AND THE YOUNG ONES COME OUT AND LOOK AFTER THEMSELVES.

COCKROACHES LIVE FOR ABOUT A YEAR.

DID YOU KNOW?

By Mrs Swarn Khandpur

The Story of Coins

Around the 7th century B.C. people in Lydia, China and India began to use pieces of metal to buy goods.

Some of these pieces had stamped symbols on one side and some on both.

These early coins were of various shapes.

The Lydian coins, made of an alloy of gold and silver were bean-shaped. The Chinese coin made of bronze was in the shape of a knife.

The Indian coins were cut from silver sheets and were of different shapes.

By the 5th century B.C. several other countries had started using coins to trade among themselves.

This made the Chinese say that money which was meant to roll around the world should itself be round.

And so by 300 B.C. they minted a round coin which remained in circulation till the beginning of this century.

Gradually other countries took to minting circular coins. Today most coins all over the world, are round.

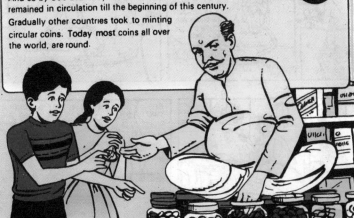

The Flying Pot

Illustrations: M. Mohandas

Based on a story sent by Vijay Kewalramani, New Kandla

Readers' Choice

AN OLD COUPLE, ONCE LIVED AT THE EDGE OF A FOREST.

I HAVEN'T SEEN OUR GRANDSON IN AGES!

WHY DON'T YOU VISIT HIM TODAY?

GOOD IDEA! I'LL TAKE HIM SOME FRUITS AND SWEETS.

SO THE OLD LADY PACKED SOME FRUITS AND SWEETS...

...AND WENT TO LOOK FOR TRANSPORT. BUT TO HER DISMAY—

YOU WANT TO CROSS THE FOREST? SORRY, IT'S TOO DANGEROUS.

THERE'S A LION ON THE PROWL.

SHE RETURNED HOME TO FIND HER HUSBAND SEATED ON A LARGE EARTHEN POT.

WHILE YOU WERE AWAY, A SADHU CAME BY. I GAVE HIM SOME FOOD AND IN RETURN HE GAVE ME THIS MAGIC POT.

A MAGIC POT? WHAT DOES IT DO?

WATCH!

POT, TAKE ME TO MY BED!

SEE THAT!

WHY, THAT'S WONDERFUL! I CAN CROSS THE FOREST ON THIS POT!

120

121

THE BOY THREW AN OLD STRINGLESS COT OVER THE WELL...

... AND SPREAD A SHEET OVER IT.

WHEN HIS GRANDMOTHER AND THE LION ARRIVED—

WELCOME, GRANDMA! I SEE WE HAVE A GUEST.

PLEASE SIR, WON'T YOU SIT HERE?

THANK YOU, BOY.

A-A-A-A-A!!

HAPPY LANDING!

NOW, GRANDMA, HAVE YOU BROUGHT SWEETS FOR ME?

HERE YOU ARE, MY PET.

AFTER HER VISIT THE OLD WOMAN RETURNED HOME ON THE POT.

HUSBAND, I'M BACK!

122

124

It Pays to be Polite

Illustrations: V. B. Halbe

Based on a story sent by Desh Raj Ashish, Patna

IT'S A TRAMP COME TO BEG.

DON'T YOU KNOW IT'S WRONG TO BEG? GO AWAY!

I HAVEN'T COME TO BEG, MADAM.

I WAS WONDERING IF YOU COULD LEND ME SOME THREAD...

...TO MEND MY SHORTS.

BUT, OF COURSE, I CAN!

HERE YOU ARE.

I WONDER WHAT HE WANTS NOW.

SORRY TO TROUBLE YOU, MADAM...

...BUT I'LL HAVE TO PATCH THESE SHORTS. I NEED A SMALL PIECE OF CLOTH.

WAIT!

HERE YOU ARE, SON.

IT'S THAT POLITE BOY AGAIN.

127

129

SHAMU SAVES HIS HEAD

Illustrations : Ashok Dongre

Based on a story sent by Sheila D'Souza.

SHAMU WAS A SIMPLETON AND PEOPLE WERE ALWAYS LAUGHING AT HIM.

AT LAST HE COULD BEAR IT NO LONGER.

I'LL GO TO THE KING AND ASK HIM WHAT I SHOULD DO?

HE WENT TO THE KING AND EXPLAINED HIS PROBLEM. THE COURTIERS WERE AMUSED.

HA! HA!

THIS IS TOO FUNNY FOR WORDS!

SILENCE!

I CAN HELP YOU. BUT YOU MUST BE PREPARED TO PAY A HEAVY PRICE.

I'LL PAY WITH MY LIFE, IF NECESSARY!

YES, YOU'LL PAY WITH YOUR LIFE IF YOU FAIL. NOW LISTEN...

130

BLACK HOLES

Script : J D Isloor
Illustrations : Anand Mande

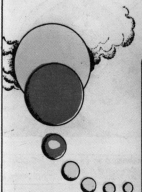

NOTHING LASTS FOREVER, NOT EVEN STARS. A STAR SHINES BRIGHTLY BECAUSE HYDROGEN NUCLEI AT ITS CENTRE ARE CONTINUOUSLY JOINING TO RELEASE TREMENDOUS AMOUNTS OF HEAT AND LIGHT.

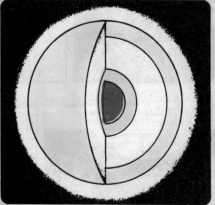

EVENTUALLY THE STAR RUNS OUT OF HYDROGEN AND OTHER FUELS.

WHEN THIS HAPPENS SOME STARS FLARE UP INTO A RED GIANT.

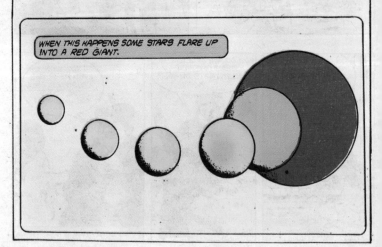

THE RED GIANT IS UNSTABLE. IT PUFFS OFF ITS OUTER LAYERS AND THESE DRIFT OFF INTO SPACE LOOKING LIKE HUGE SMOKE RINGS. SUCH A RING IS CALLED A NEBULA.
FINALLY, ALL THAT IS LEFT IS A VERY DENSE WHITE DWARF STAR. THIS SLOWLY COOLS DOWN UNTIL IT IS ONLY A COLD DARK CINDER IN SPACE.

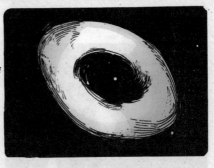

IN THE CASE OF SOME GIANT STARS, A VIOLENT EXPLOSION MAY TAKE PLACE.

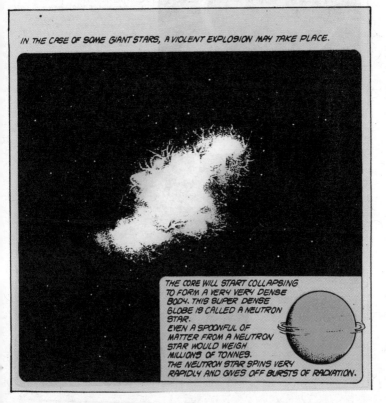

THE CORE WILL START COLLAPSING TO FORM A VERY VERY DENSE BODY. THIS SUPER DENSE GLOBE IS CALLED A NEUTRON STAR.
EVEN A SPOONFUL OF MATTER FROM A NEUTRON STAR WOULD WEIGH MILLIONS OF TONNES.
THE NEUTRON STAR SPINS VERY RAPIDLY AND GIVES OFF BURSTS OF RADIATION.

ARTIST'S IMPRESSION OF A BLACK HOLE.
A BLACK HOLE CANNOT BE SEEN.

SOME STARS SHRINK EVEN FURTHER AND END UP AS BLACK HOLES.
IN A BLACK HOLE A HUGE AMOUNT OF MATTER IS HEAVILY COMPRESSED INTO A VERY SMALL SPACE.
THE BLACK HOLE HAS SUCH A TREMENDOUS GRAVITATIONAL PULL THAT IT SUCKS IN ANYTHING THAT GOES NEAR IT...
AND ANYTHING THAT GOES INSIDE A BLACK HOLE NEVER COMES OUT AGAIN. IT IS LOST FOREVER.
A BLACK HOLE DOESN'T EVEN LET LIGHT COME OUT OF IT. SO WE CANNOT SEE A BLACK HOLE. IT IS TOTALLY INVISIBLE.

TODAY SOME SCIENTISTS BELIEVE THAT THERE MAY BE HUGE BLACK HOLES AT THE CENTRE OF MOST GALAXIES, INCLUDING OUR OWN MILKY WAY, DEVOURING ENTIRE STARS AT A GULP.

134

Cheats will surely be cheated

Script : Navina Venkat ■ Illustrations : S.N. Sawant

ISUKA, A POOR MAN FROM YACHAVANA, SET OFF FOR ANOTHER VILLAGE.

PEDAKA FROM MACHAVANA ALSO WANTED TO MAKE HIS FORTUNE IN ANOTHER VILLAGE.

ON THE WAY BOTH STOPPED TO REST UNDER THE SAME BANYAN TREE.

I'M HUNGRY. THAT MUST BE A BUNDLE OF FOOD HE HAS GOT.

WHAT DOES YOUR BUNDLE CONTAIN?

ER... RICE.

BUT I WOULD HAVE PREFERRED VEGETABLES.

WHAT A COINCIDENCE! I HAVE VEGETABLES BUT I PREFER RICE.

136

THE ADVENTURES OF SUPPANDI - 8

Based on a story sent by Padam G. Kriplani, Thane

Illustrations: Ram Waeerkar

ONCE SUPPANDI, THE VILLAGE SIMPLETON, TOOK A JOB AS A SERVANT WITH A LOCAL LANDLORD.

ONE DAY, WHEN THE LANDLORD HAD A GUEST—

HEY, SUPPANDI!

GET ME A TELESCOPE FROM THE CUPBOARD.

SUPPANDI SCURRIED OFF...

... AND SOON—

HERE YOU ARE, SIR.

WHEN THE GUEST HAD LEFT—

IDIOT! BEFORE GOING TO FETCH THE TELESCOPE YOU SHOULD'VE ASKED ME WHICH ONE I WANTED...

...THE ENGLISH ONE OR THE JAPANESE ONE! THE GUEST WOULD'VE KNOWN THAT I AM RICH.

YES, SIR. I'M SORRY.

SOME DAYS LATER, THE LANDLORD HAD ANOTHER GUEST—

ER... WHO KILLED THIS STAG?

MY FATHER.

HE WAS A GREAT HUNTER! OH, YOU SHOULD'VE SEEN HIM!

SUPPANDI, BRING ONE OF MY FATHER'S PHOTOGRAPHS!

WHICH FATHER, SIR? YOUR ENGLISH FATHER OR YOUR JAPANESE FATHER?

HOW THE MICE BELLED THE CAT

Illustrations: Ashok Dongre

Story sent by Dominic D'Costa, Bombay

ONCE, A CAT HAPPENED TO COME UPON A PEACEFUL COLONY OF MICE.

SNEAKING SLOWLY FORWARD, IT POUNCED UPON THEM.

EEEK!

EEEK!

HELP! HELP!

THE POOR MICE LOST MANY OF THEIR RELATIVES AND FRIENDS.

LATER, THE MICE CALLED AN EMERGENCY MEETING.

WHEN THE CAT COMES AGAIN, WE MUST NOT BE CAUGHT IN THE OPEN.

BUT HOW WILL WE KNOW THE CAT IS COMING?

ANY SUGGESTIONS?

N... NOTHING GOOD ENOUGH.

IN A CORNER SAT AN OLD MOUSE.

DON'T WORRY, YOUNG ONES. I'LL TELL YOU WHAT TO DO.

TELL US, GRANDPA, TELL US.

SO THE OLD MOUSE TOLD THEM

140

THE CAT SHOT FORWARD.

I HAVE WON! I HAVE WON!

(HUFF)...(PUFF)...(PUFF) CAT, WE AGREE. YOU'RE MUCH FASTER THAN WE COULD EVER BE.

AND NOW— THE PRIZE!

WHAT IS IT?

A SHINING, GOLDEN BELL.

THE MICE WERE OVERJOYED. NOW THEY WOULD ALWAYS HEAR THE CAT WHENEVER IT APPROACHED.

THANK YOU, DEAR GRANDPA.

THANK YOU, DEAR DOG AND BIRD. YOU HAVE SAVED OUR LIVES.

143

144

Let's make moving pictures

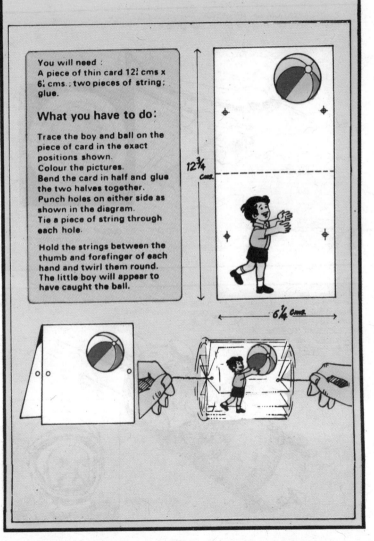

You will need :
A piece of thin card 12¾ cms x
6¼ cms.; two pieces of string;
glue.

What you have to do:

Trace the boy and ball on the
piece of card in the exact
positions shown.
Colour the pictures.
Bend the card in half and glue
the two halves together.
Punch holes on either side as
shown in the diagram.
Tie a piece of string through
each hole.

Hold the strings between the
thumb and forefinger of each
hand and twirl them round.
The little boy will appear to
have caught the ball.

12¾ cms.

6¼ cms.

The Saga of Spaceships

Script : J.D. Isloor
Illustrations : Anand Mande

WITH THE INVENTION OF THE AEROPLANE, MAN COULD FLY FROM ONE END OF THE EARTH TO THE OTHER.

BUT HE COULD NOT LEAVE THE PLANET AND GO OFF INTO OUTER SPACE. THIS WAS BECAUSE AEROPLANE ENGINES NEED AIR TO FUNCTION AND THERE IS NO AIR ABOVE 960 KM. FROM THE EARTH'S SURFACE.

IT WAS AN ASTOUNDING FEAT THEREFORE, WHEN ON APRIL 12, 1964, YURI GAGARIN HURTLED INTO OUTER SPACE IN THE SPACESHIP VOSTOK, AND CIRCLED THE EARTH IN JUST 108 MINUTES.

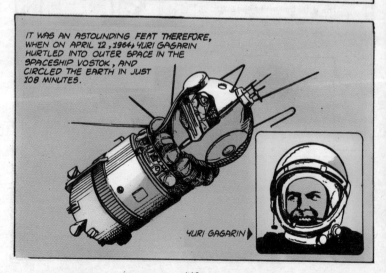

YURI GAGARIN ▶

WE NEED POWERFUL ROCKETS TO SEND SPACESHIPS INTO SPACE. THE BASIC PRINCIPLE OF THE WORKING OF A ROCKET IS VERY SIMPLE. IT CAN BE EASILY ILLUSTRATED WITH THE HELP OF A BALLOON.

BLOW UP A BALLOON AND SUDDENLY LEAVE IT ...

...IT FLIES AWAY AS IT REDUCES TO ITS ORIGINAL SIZE. AS THE AIR FROM THE BALLOON GUSHES OUT FROM THE NOZZLE, THE REACTION PUSHES THE BALLOON FORWARD.

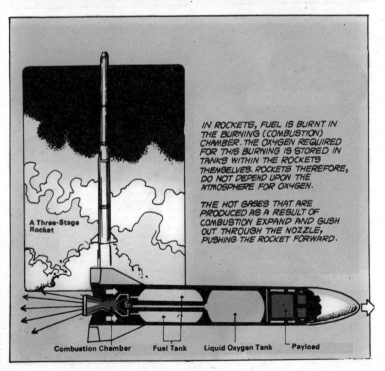

A Three-Stage Rocket

IN ROCKETS, FUEL IS BURNT IN THE BURNING (COMBUSTION) CHAMBER. THE OXYGEN REQUIRED FOR THIS BURNING IS STORED IN TANKS WITHIN THE ROCKETS THEMSELVES. ROCKETS THEREFORE, DO NOT DEPEND UPON THE ATMOSPHERE FOR OXYGEN.

THE HOT GASES THAT ARE PRODUCED AS A RESULT OF COMBUSTION EXPAND AND GUSH OUT THROUGH THE NOZZLE, PUSHING THE ROCKET FORWARD.

Combustion Chamber   Fuel Tank   Liquid Oxygen Tank   Payload

JET AEROPLANES TOO, WORK ON THE SAME PRINCIPLE. BUT THE MAIN DIFFERENCE BETWEEN A JET AEROPLANE AND A ROCKET IS THAT THE JET ENGINES TAKE OXYGEN FROM THE AIR OR ATMOSPHERE TO BURN THE FUEL.

JET PLANES, THEREFORE, CAN WORK ONLY IN THE ATMOSPHERE WHILE ROCKETS CAN FLY IN TOTAL VACUUM AS IN OUTER SPACE.

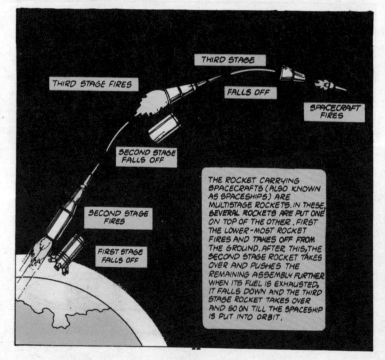

THIRD STAGE FIRES

THIRD STAGE

FALLS OFF

SPACECRAFT FIRES

SECOND STAGE FALLS OFF

SECOND STAGE FIRES

FIRST STAGE FALLS OFF

THE ROCKET CARRYING SPACECRAFTS (ALSO KNOWN AS SPACESHIPS) ARE MULTISTAGE ROCKETS. IN THESE, SEVERAL ROCKETS ARE PUT ONE ON TOP OF THE OTHER. FIRST THE LOWER-MOST ROCKET FIRES AND TAKES OFF FROM THE GROUND. AFTER THIS, THE SECOND STAGE ROCKET TAKES OVER AND PUSHES THE REMAINING ASSEMBLY FURTHER WHEN ITS FUEL IS EXHAUSTED, IT FALLS DOWN AND THE THIRD STAGE ROCKET TAKES OVER AND SO ON TILL THE SPACESHIP IS PUT INTO ORBIT.

Readers' Choice

GOPAL THE JESTER
Illustrations: S.N.Sawant

Based on a story sent by Rajesh Agrawal. Hyderabad

ONCE, GOPAL FELL ILL.

MOTHER KALI! PLEASE CURE ME.

IF YOU DO, I'LL SELL MY COW AND WHATEVER I GET FOR IT, I'LL OFFER TO YOU.

GOPAL RECOVERED FROM HIS ILLNESS. AND THEN—

WHAT A RASH PROMISE I MADE.

BUT I MUST KEEP IT... AH, I'VE AN IDEA!

COME ON, PUSSY! WE'RE GOING TO THE MARKET.

AND SOON—

COW FOR SALE! JUST ONE RUPEE!

I'LL BUY IT!

SELL IT TO ME!

150

Kalia
THE CROW

Script:
DENIS

Illustrations:
RAM WAEERKAR

151

152

153

THE RESOURCEFUL RANI

Illustrations : Dilip Kadam

LONG AGO THERE WERE TWO KINGS WHO WERE ENEMIES. ONE MORNING, AT THE PALACE OF ONE OF THEM —

I COME WITH GOOD NEWS, MAHARAJ.

OUR ENEMY HAS GONE AWAY WITH HIS ARMY TO FIGHT A BATTLE.

HE HAS LEFT JUST A HANDFUL OF MEN BEHIND TO GUARD THE FORT.

LET'S CAPTURE IT.

AND SO, BEFORE NOON, THE KING AND HIS ARMY SET OUT.

LATE IN THE EVENING—

!

WE ARE BEING INVADED!

INVADED! OH, GOD! WE HAVE ONLY A FEW ARCHERS TO PROTECT US!

HEARING THE COMMOTION, THE RANI CAME OUT.

WHAT'S ALL THE NOISE ABOUT?

THE C-CITY IS MARCHING TOWARDS... I MEAN THE C-CITY IS OUR ENEMY...

STOP CHATTERING! CALM DOWN AND SPEAK SENSE!

AN ARMY IS M-MARCHING TOWARDS OUR CITY.

OH! I SEE.

157

158

THE STETHOSCOPE

Script : N. N. Laha
Illustrations : Anand Mande

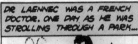

DR LAENNEC WAS A FRENCH DOCTOR. ONE DAY AS HE WAS STROLLING THROUGH A PARK...

...HE SAW SOME CHILDREN PLAYING.

KEEP THE END TO YOUR EAR.

NOW LISTEN.

TAP TAP

I CAN HEAR YOU TAPPING!

NOW YOU TAP AND I'LL LISTEN.

WHAT CLEVER CHILDREN!

SOME DAYS LATER A WOMAN CAME TO SEE DR LAENNEC.

DOCTOR, I'M NOT WELL.

MY HEART IS BEATING IN A PECULIAR WAY.

PULSE SEEMS NORMAL.

I WISH I COULD LISTEN TO HER HEARTBEATS. BUT HOW...?

NOW YOU TAP AND I'LL LISTEN.

HMM... PERHAPS I COULD LISTEN TO HER HEARTBEATS IN THE SAME WAY.

THIS ROLL OF PAPER WILL DO JUST AS WELL AS THE ROD THEY WERE USING.

WONDERFUL! I CAN HEAR HER HEARTBEATS PERFECTLY.

DR LAENNEC HAD INVENTED THE FIRST STETHOSCOPE. LATER HE BEGAN TO USE A WOODEN TUBE INSTEAD OF A ROLL OF PAPER.

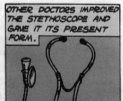

OTHER DOCTORS IMPROVED THE STETHOSCOPE AND GAVE IT ITS PRESENT FORM.

DOCTORS USE THE STETHOSCOPE TO LISTEN TO A PERSON'S HEARTBEATS AND TO OTHER SOUNDS MADE IN THE BODY.

A WOLF SINGS!

Illustrations: Ashok Dongre

READERS' CHOICE

Based on a story sent by G.S. Ramakrishna, Hyderabad

A SHEEP WAS WANDERING THROUGH A FOREST...

...WHEN SUDDENLY—

AH, YOU TASTY, JUICY MORSEL! I'M GOING TO EAT YOU UP!

OH SIR, BEFORE YOU DO, PLEASE SING ME A SONG SO THAT I CAN DIE HAPPILY.

ALL RIGHT— HERE GOES!

Tra la la la dumpty eh...screech! Tra la la la scrumpty eh... screech!

NEAR BY—

WHAT A DREADFUL DIN.

IT SOUNDS LIKE A WOLF.

LET'S DRIVE HIM AWAY!

AND SO—

BANG! CRASH! BASH!

THE WOLF RAN FOR HIS LIFE...

...AND THE SHEEP QUICKLY RETURNED HOME.

GREEN GOLD

Illustrations : Dilip Kadam

Based on a story sent by Eren Rosario, Goa

Readers' Choice

SISTER...

GIVE ME TEN PAISE, SISTER...

TEN PAISE? NO! I'LL GIVE HER SOMETHING ELSE.

I WON'T GIVE YOU MONEY...TAKE THESE PLANTS INSTEAD.

GROW THEM WITH CARE, AND YOU WILL BE REPAID A HUNDRED-FOLD!

WHEN THE BEGGAR-GIRL REACHED HER HOME...

THERE YOU ARE, CHAMPA! HOW MUCH DID YOU GET TODAY?

MOTHER, I HAD NO LUCK TODAY. A GIRL GAVE ME SOME PLANTS AND THAT'S ALL I GOT.

PLANTS? THEY ARE OF NO USE!

I AM SURE THE GIRL MEANT WELL. I'LL GIVE THESE PLANTS ALL MY LOVE AND CARE.

CHAMPA PLANTED THE SAPLINGS...

...AND TENDED THEM WITH LOVING CARE. A FEW DAYS LATER—

HOW WELL THEY ARE GROWING.

CHAMPA BEGAN TO SPEND A GREAT DEAL OF TIME WITH HER PLANTS...

...AND GRADUALLY, INSTEAD OF GOING TO BEG FOR MONEY...

...SHE BEGAN TO ASK AROUND FOR SEEDS AND SAPLINGS.

VERY SOON FLOWERS OF ALL SORTS BEGAN TO BLOOM IN HER BACKYARD.

WHAT A PRETTY GARDEN.

164

166

168

THE MERCHANT AND THE PARROT

Illustrations: Souren Roy

Readers' Choice

Based on a story sent by Suchandra Bhattacharya, Shillong

A MERCHANT HAD A TALKING PARROT. ONE DAY —

HIRAMAN, I AM GOING TO BENGAL ON A BUSINESS TRIP.

DO ME A FAVOUR.

GET THE PARROTS OF BENGAL TO TELL YOU THE SECRET OF ESCAPING FROM A CAGE.

DO YOU THINK I WOULD TELL YOU THE SECRET EVEN IF THEY TOLD IT TO ME?

I LOVE YOU TOO MUCH TO LET YOU GO.

BUT PLEASE ASK THEM.

SETHJI WENT TO BENGAL. ONE DAY HE SAW SOME PARROTS ON A TREE.

OH! MY PROMISE TO MY PARROT.

O GREEN-FEATHERED FRIENDS! I WANT TO KNOW SOMETHING FROM YOU.

MY HIRAMAN, WHO LIVES IN A CAGE, WANTS TO KNOW HOW TO ESCAPE.

HEARING THIS A PARROT FELL DEAD.

WHEN THE MERCHANT RETURNED HOME—

DID YOU ASK THE PARROTS?

YES.

BUT WHEN I DID SO, ONE OF THEM FELL DEAD ON THE SPOT.

OH!

POOR HIRAMAN! I KNEW HE WAS TOO SOFT-HEARTED TO HEAR SUCH SAD NEWS.

?

THAT PARROT IN BENGAL DID NOT REALLY DIE, YOU KNOW...

HE MERELY ACTED OUT THE TRICK I SHOULD PLAY ON YOU.

YOU PARROTS ARE INDEED VERY CLEVER.

WELL, GOODBYE MY FRIEND.

THE MERCHANT AND THE TAILOR

Script:
Luis M. Fernandes

Illustrations:
Ram Waeerkar

A RICH MERCHANT WENT TO A TAILOR WITH A PIECE OF CLOTH.

MAKE ME A CAP WILL YOU?

CERTAINLY, SIR.

THE TAILOR SEEMED VERY PLEASED... I WONDER WHY?

PERHAPS THE CLOTH IS BIG ENOUGH FOR TWO CAPS... YES, THAT MUST BE IT.

ER... LOOK HERE, MAKE TWO CAPS OUT OF THAT CLOTH.

ALL RIGHT, SIR.

HE DIDN'T BAT AN EYELID. PERHAPS THE CLOTH IS BIG ENOUGH FOR THREE CAPS.

I WANT THREE CAPS, NOT TWO.

ANYTHING YOU SAY.

IF HE CAN MAKE THREE CAPS OUT OF THAT CLOTH, WHY NOT FOUR!

MAKE IT FOUR.

AS YOU WISH, SIR!

172

THE MERCHANT KEPT GOING BACK TO THE SHOP. TILL FINALLY—

I WANT TEN CAPS MADE OUT OT THAT CLOTH.

THEY'LL BE READY TOMORROW EVENING, SIR.

I'VE GOT THE BETTER OF HIM! I DON'T THINK MUCH CLOTH COULD BE LEFT OVER AFTER HE HAS MADE THOSE TEN CAPS.

AND NOW I CAN WEAR A NEW CAP EACH DAY FOR TEN DAYS.

THE FOLLOWING EVENING—

ARE THE CAPS READY?

YES.

HERE YOU ARE, SIR.

WHAT?

YOU ASKED ME TO MAKE TEN CAPS OUT OF THAT PIECE OF CLOTH, SIR. HERE THEY ARE. NOW PLEASE PAY ME.

THE MERCHANT WENT AWAY A SADDER BUT WISER MAN.

TANTRI THE MANTRI

Script: Iyer Prasad B.
Illustrations: Ashok Dongre

I WONDER WHY THE PEOPLE ARE CROWDING OVER THERE?

GRROW!!

GET OUT OF MY WAY.

WHAT HAVE YOU GOT THERE?

A FEROCIOUS LEOPARD, SIR. I CAUGHT IT MYSELF.

A FEROCIOUS LEOPARD! THE BEAST COULD GET ME ON THE THRONE!

CLEAR OUT, ALL OF YOU.

HOW MUCH DO YOU WANT FOR IT?

A THOUSAND RUPEES.

DONE. THERE'S THE MONEY. HAVE HIM SENT TO THE PALACE.

174

175

This story by Sigrun O. Srivastava won the Second Prize in the Tinkle Original Story Competition.

THE GREATEST SHOW ON EARTH

Illustrations : V.B. Halbe

IN THE VILLAGE OF KRISHNAPUR LIVED A BOY NAMED TUTU. TUTU HAD MANY FRIENDS, BUT HIS BEST FRIENDS WERE BOO, THE OLD BUFFALO ON HIS FATHER'S FARM...

... AND HIS CLASSMATE, LASSI. ONE MORNING —

LASSI, LASSI, LISTEN ! OH WAKE UP, LASSI !

AAAH...

WHY, TUTU, WHAT HAS HAPPENED?

IT'S BOO, OUR BOO...

FATHER HAS GIVEN HIM ONLY ONE MONTH'S TIME TO STAY ON AT THE FARM. AFTER THAT, HE SAYS THAT I WILL HAVE TO ABANDON BOO IN THE FOREST.

I KNOW BOO IS OLD AND CANNOT WORK ANYMORE, BUT TO LEAVE HIM IN THE FOREST...! HE'LL BE LOST AND FRIEND-LESS THERE.

TUTU, WE'LL NOT LET THAT HAPPEN. COME, LET'S THINK OF SOMETHING THAT WILL HELP SAVE BOO.

DO YOU THINK WE COULD TEACH HIM TO... TO ...

TO WHAT ?

SO TUTU TOLD HIM.

NO, IT'S IMPOSSIBLE.

177

THAT AFTERNOON, THE TWO BOYS, MOUNTED ON BOO'S BACK, RODE DOWN TO THE RIVER BANK.

AND THERE..

NOW, LISTEN TO ME, BOO. WE ARE GOING TO TEACH YOU HOW TO DANCE.

MONKEYS, HORSES AND DOGS LEARN TO DANCE, THEN WHY NOT YOU?

COME ON, LASSI GIVE HIM THE BEAT. AND YOU BOO, WATCH ME.

COME ON BOO, LOOK AT MY FEET.

THRUM THRUM DHUM

TAP TAP TAP TAP

DID YOU GET THAT, BOO?

178

BOO STARED GRAVELY AT TUTU. THEN —

AAAH!

OH, COME ON NOW! PAY ATTENTION, BOO. LET'S TRY AGAIN.

COME ON, TRY.

DHRUM DHRUM DHRUM DHRUM

YAP

YOU CAN DO IT. I'M SURE YOU CAN.

BUT BOO JUST LOWERED HIS HEAD AND BEGAN TO CROP THE GRASS.

BOO, PLEASE LOOK AT ME. I'LL LIFT YOUR LEGS FOR YOU...

...THIS WAY, THAT WAY; THIS WAY, THAT WAY. NOW AGAIN!

SO LASSI STARTED TO BEAT THE DRUM AGAIN AND TUTU DANCED, BUT BOO DID NOT MOVE AN INCH!

TUTU, IT'S NO USE. I GIVE UP.

TUTU TURNED TO LASSI, TEARS GLISTENED IN HIS EYES.

OH LASSI, NO! WE HAVE TO TEACH HIM. HE HAS TO LEARN IT. THAT'S THE ONLY CHANCE WE'VE GOT.

THE FRIENDS TAUGHT BOO THE WHOLE AFTERNOON AND ALL THROUGH THE NEXT DAY AND THE WHOLE WEEK.

BUT BOO DID NOT LIFT HIS FEET.

TUTU, I GIVE UP. IT'S HOPELESS. THE FELLOW IS TOO STUPID TO LEARN ANYTHING.

LET'S GO HOME!

AND THE NEXT MOMENT—

LASSI, LASSI LOOK.

ZING!

181

SO TEARING FOUR PAGES OUT OF THEIR OLD COPY BOOKS, LASSI BROUGHT OUT HIS RED AND BLUE INK PENS AND SET TO WORK.

THAT'S IT!

THE GREATEST SHOW ON EARTH! BOO THE WONDER BUFFALO SHOWS HIS WONDERFUL TRICKS! IT IS UNBELIEVABLE, BUT TRUE! FIRST SHOW ON SUNDAY AT 4 O'CLOCK UNDER THE THREE BANYAN TREES! ENTRANCE 20 PAISA! ALL ARE WELCOME! DONATIONS ARE WELCOME TOO!

I WISH I COULD ADD 'ART AND MUSIC DIRECTOR: LASSI KATTA SINGH', BUT THERE IS NO SPACE LEFT.

THE TWO FRIENDS PASTED THE FIRST POSTER BY THE SCHOOL DOOR (WHEN THE TEACHER WAS NOT AROUND!), THE SECOND ON THE POST-BOX; THE THIRD IN KUNTIL MANDAL'S RICE SHOP AND THE FOURTH AT THE PAANWALLAH'S SHOP.

AND THAT SUNDAY...

182

HOW WONDERFUL BOO LOOKED AS THE BOYS MARCHED HIM PROUDLY DOWN TO THE THREE BANYAN TREES!

AND WHAT A CROWD HAD GATHERED! ALMOST EVERYBODY IN KRISHNAPUR WAS THERE.

HERE THEY COME! HURRAH! WHAT CAN THE WONDER BUFFALO DO?

PERHAPS HE CAN LAY A GOLD EGG!

HA, HA, HA! HO, HO, HO!

TUTU IGNORED THE SHOUTS OF LAUGHTER. THEN —

SILENCE PLEASE! THE PERFORMANCE WILL NOW BEGIN.

BOO, BOO, DO YOUR BEST. DANCE, DANCE!

BUT BOO STOOD MOTIONLESS AND GAZED AT THE CROWD.

THEN SLOWLY, HE RAISED HIS HOOF AND —

THE PEOPLE OF KRISHNAPUR HELD THEIR BREATH. THEY COULDN'T BELIEVE THEIR EYES!

THEN EVERYONE BURST INTO APPLAUSE! THE PAANWALLAH, THE POSTMAN, KUNTIL MANDAL FROM THE RICE-SHOP AND EVEN THE SCHOOL-TEACHER, CHEERED.

THEN TUTU CAME FORWARD.

ATTENTION! BOO WILL NOW BALANCE A BALL ON THE TIP OF HIS NOSE.

THE CROWD GASPED.

IMPOSSIBLE! NO BUFFALO CAN DO THAT.

BOO CAN!

NO, HE CANNOT!

EVERYONE TURNED TO SEE WHO HAD SPOKEN. IT WAS GURBACHAN SINGH, THE RICHEST FARMER IN THE VILLAGE.

NO BUFFALO HAS DONE IT AND NO BUFFALO EVER WILL. I CAN BET ON IT.

THERE WAS PIN-DROP SILENCE. THEN TUTU CLEARED HIS THROAT.

I ACCEPT THE BET.

GOOD!

AND THEY SHOOK HANDS ON IT.

TUTU'S HEART WAS IN HIS MOUTH AS HE WENT TO BOO.

I COUNT ON YOU TO DO IT. DON'T DROP THE BALL. FOR YOUR SAKE AND MINE, DON'T DROP IT.

BOO RAISED HIS HEAD.

START, BOO!

THE CROWD CLAPPED AND WHISTLED...

GOOD SHOW!

WE WANT MORE!

... WHILE GURBACHAN SHOOK HIS HEAD OVER AND OVER AGAIN IN DISBELIEF.

THEN HE QUIETLY PRESSED A NOTE INTO TUTU'S HAND.

BUY BOO SOME OILCAKES FOR HIS DINNER TONIGHT.

THEN TUTU GOT UP ON A BUCKET.

FRIENDS, AS YOU HAVE SEEN, BOO IS VERY CLEVER, BUT HE IS VERY OLD AND USELESS FOR WORK.

186

THE MONEYLENDER MEETS HIS MATCH

Illustrations Ram Waeerkar

Based on a story sent by Arup Jyoti, Nageland

WHEN THE MAN HAD CLIMBED UP —

NOW LISTEN — FOR A MONTH NOW, I HAVE BEEN THE KEEPER OF THIS BUFFALO.

MY JOB IS MERELY TO SIT ON THIS TREE AND MIND IT. WHEN I TAKE IT BACK TO THE PALACE IN THE EVENING, THE KING GIVES ME A THOUSAND GOLD COINS.

A THOUSAND GOLD COINS? FOR ONLY A DAY'S WORK?

YES — THAT'S HOW PRECIOUS THIS BUFFALO IS!

HAVING DONE THIS JOB FOR SO LONG, I HAVE BECOME A RICH MAN.

NOW I FEEL I SHOULD LET SOMEBODY ELSE MAKE SOME MONEY TOO.

HOW THOUGHTFUL AND KIND YOU ARE! I WILL GLADLY TAKE UP THE JOB!

A WISE DECISION!

THE BRUTE IS STILL ASLEEP. GOOD!

AS QUIETLY AS HE COULD THE WOODCUTTER CLIMBED DOWN THE TREE.

I MUST SIT ALL DAY ON THIS TREE, YOU SAID?

SSSH... SSH ...YES, YES, OR YOU WON'T GET YOUR GOLD COINS.

SO ALL AFTERNOON, THE MONEY LENDER SAT ON THE TREE.

OOOH! HOW STIFF AND SORE MY LIMBS HAVE BECOME.

FINALLY, IN THE EVENING, HE CLIMBED DOWN.

GET UP, YOU! I WANT MY GOLD COINS.

GRRAH...!

OW!

AAAH! HE'LL GORE ME TO DEATH.

HELP!

IT WAS A LONG TIME BEFORE THE BUFFALO LEFT...

...AND THE TERRIFIED MAN COULD CLIMB DOWN AGAIN.

I... I NEVER WANT TO SEE A BUFFALO AGAIN!

You can't Fool Chachaji

Illustrations: Ashok Dongra

This story by Margaret Bhatty won the Consolation Prize in the Tinkle Original Story Competition.

IT WAS APRIL FOOL'S DAY, ASHA, DHIREN AND THEIR BELOVED CHACHAJI SAT ROUND THE TABLE.

OH, THE JOKES WE PLAYED ON APRIL FOOL'S DAY, WHEN I WAS YOUNG! THEY WERE FULL OF WIT AND IMAGINATION.

WHAT'S THE MATTER? WHY ARE YOU STARING AT ME?

THERE IS A SMUDGE ON YOUR CHIN, CHACHAJI.

HA! HA! THAT IS A VERY STALE ONE, SON. YOU WILL HAVE TO BE SMARTER TO FOOL YOUR OLD CHACHAJI.

JUST THEN THE CHILDREN'S MOTHER CAME INTO THE ROOM.

THERE IS A SMUDGE ON YOUR CHIN, CHACHAJI.

THERE IS?

OOPS! IT MUST HAVE GOT THERE WHILE I WAS POLISHING MY SHOES.

HA! HA! WE TOLD YOU SO CHACHAJI.

AH, WELL I MUST BE OFF TO THE COURT.

193

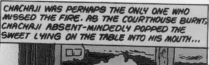

CHACHAJI WAS PERHAPS THE ONLY ONE WHO MISSED THE FIRE. AS THE COURTHOUSE BURNT, CHACHAJI ABSENT-MINDEDLY POPPED THE SWEET LYING ON THE TABLE INTO HIS MOUTH...

...AND SPAT IT OUT IN DISGUST.

IT WAS SOAP!

194

TANTRI
THE MANTRI

Script: Dev Nadkarni
Illustrations: Ashok Dongre

THE WEATHER IS VERY WARM, ISN'T IT, TANTRI?

YES, YOUR MAJESTY, MUCH TOO WARM.

I THINK I'LL SPEND THE WEEK-END ALONE IN MY HOUSEBOAT ON THE LAKE.

AN EXCELLENT IDEA!

A FEW DAYS LATER—

THE KING LEAVES TOMORROW AND I HAVEN'T EVEN PLANNED HOW TO PREVENT HIS RETURN!

HOW DOES ONE SINK A HOUSEBOAT IN THE CENTRE OF A LAKE?

I HAVE IT!

THE NEXT DAY—

...AND TAKE GOOD CARE OF AFFAIRS WHILE I'M AWAY...

YOU CAN TRUST ME.

THAT DOES IT!

THE ADVENTURES OF SUPPANDI-5

Illustrations: Ram Waeerkar   Based on a story sent by K. Bhagatchandra Singh, Goa

ONE DAY, SUPPANDI WENT TO TOWN LOOKING FOR WORK.

SIR, THAT TIN SEEMS HEAVY. DO YOU NEED SOMEONE TO CARRY IT?

YES, I DO. BUT THERE'S COOKING OIL IN IT. BE CAREFUL NOT TO SPILL IT.

ON THE WAY—

AH! AN AMLA TREE!

AS THEY WERE PASSING A POND—

I'LL DRINK SOME WATER.

MMM! THIS WATER IS SO SWEET!*

* WATER DRUNK AFTER EATING AMLA, TASTES SWEET

198

THE BASHFUL SON-IN-LAW

Script:
Gayatri Madan Dutt

Illustrations:
Ram Waeerkar

ONCE, A MAN KNOWN FOR HIS EXTREME SHYNESS, SET OUT FOR HIS MOTHER-IN-LAW'S HOUSE. HE TOOK A BARBER ALONG FOR COMPANY.

THEY WERE GIVEN A CORDIAL WELCOME.

WHAT A LOVELY SURPRISE! COME, YOU ARE JUST IN TIME FOR LUNCH.

UM! DELICIOUS RICE AND PICKLE!

PLEASE BEGIN. I'LL SIT BY TO SERVE YOU.

THE BARBER AT ONCE FELL UPON HIS FOOD WITH GUSTO...

...BUT THE SON-IN-LAW DID NOT.

WHAT'S WRONG?

203

204

THE NEXT MINUTE...

SON-IN-LAW...

ULP!

... THE OTHERS FEEL THAT YOU MAY HAVE A TUMMY-UPSET. IS THAT WHAT'S WRONG?

OH! WHAT IS IT, MY CHILD?

HOW CAN I MUNCH IN FRONT OF HER?

SPEAK TO ME, CHILD. SPEAK!

BUT MY MOUTH'S FULL.

HE CAN'T SPEAK! AND LOOK— HIS CHEEKS ARE SWOLLEN...

207

HE COUNTED BEFORE EATING

A folktale from Goa

Script:
Luis M. Fernandes

Illustrations:
Ram Waeerkar

A SON-IN LAW ON A VISIT TO HIS WIFE'S HOUSE HAD JUST AWAKENED FROM HIS AFTERNOON SIESTA.

I COULD DO WITH SOME TEA NOW.

SAOANSOAN....!

OH, THEY'RE FRYING SANNAS!*

MMM... I CAN HARDLY WAIT TO EAT THEM.

SOAONSANN

THAT'S TWO! I'LL COUNT HOW MANY THEY MAKE.

THEY MUST BE TAKING IT OUT OF THE PAN NOW.

SOAONSOANN!

THAT'S THREE.

IN THE KITCHEN— IT'S DONE ON THAT SIDE. TURN IT OVER.

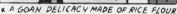

* A GOAN DELICACY MADE OF RICE FLOUR

208

THAT'S FOUR.

THE SON-IN-LAW DID NOT KNOW THAT HE WAS COUNTING EACH SANNA TWICE. AND FINALLY—

THEY HAVE MADE TEN. WONDERFUL!

AT TEA-TIME, THE WIFE'S YOUNGER BROTHER PUSHED IN TO GRAB A SANNA, BUT—

NOT NOW! PEDRO! LET YOUR BROTHER-IN-LAW EAT FIRST.

GO AND CALL HIM FOR TEA.

THE SON-IN-LAW CAME EAGERLY TO THE TABLE...

...AND BEGAN TO EAT.

DELICIOUS!

WHILE THE LITTLE BOY WATCHED FROM THE DOORWAY.

THAT'S ONE.

The Telephone

Script:
Subba Rao

Illustrations:
Anand Mande

GRAHAM BELL WAS WORKING WITH AN INSTRUMENT DESIGNED TO CARRY SOUND, IN HIS WORKSHOP IN BOSTON, AMERICA.

BY ACCIDENT HE SPILLED SOME BATTERY ACID ON HIS TROUSERS.

HE GOT UP AND CRIED OUT—

WATSON...

...PLEASE COME HERE. I WANT YOU!

WATSON, BELL'S ASSISTANT, WORKING IN ANOTHER ROOM ON THE FIRST FLOOR, WAS STUNNED BECAUSE HIS EMPLOYER'S VOICE HAD COME THROUGH THE INSTRUMENT!

HE RAN DOWN THE STAIRS ...

...AND BURST INTO BELL'S ROOM.

IT WORKS! IT WORKS!

THE ERA OF THE TELEPHONE HAD BEGUN. THE YEAR WAS 1876.

IN THE EARLY MODELS THE SAME TUBE SERVED AS THE MOUTHPIECE AND THE EARPIECE. ANYONE USING THE TELEPHONE HAD TO BE EXTREMELY AGILE, MOVING HIS EAR AND MOUTH TO THE INSTRUMENT TO HEAR AND SPEAK ALTERNATELY.
ONE MODEL CARRIED THE NOTICE:
"DO NOT LISTEN WITH YOUR MOUTH AND TALK WITH YOUR EAR."

IN LATER MODELS, THE EARPIECE AND THE MOUTHPIECE WERE SEPARATED BUT ONE HAD TO SHOUT. TO MAKE ONESELF HEARD ON THE TELEPHONE...

...TILL DAVID HUGHES CAME UP WITH THE MICROPHONE, AND IT WAS COMBINED WITH THE LISTENING TUBE.

HERE ARE PICTURES OF VARIOUS MODELS OF THE TELEPHONE DEVELOPED OVER THE YEARS.

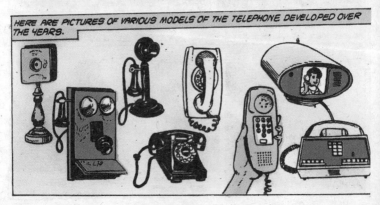

ON NOVEMBER 18, 1881 AT THE BANDSTAND ON THE SOUTH BEACH, MADRAS, THE GOVERNOR'S BAND PLAYED A VARIETY OF PIECES...

...WHICH A NUMBER OF PEOPLE LISTENED TO WITH DELIGHT AT THE MESS HOUSE AT FORT ST GEORGE.

THE TELEPHONE HAD ARRIVED IN INDIA!

HOWEVER, IT WAS ONLY IN 1950, THREE YEARS AFTER THE COUNTRY BECAME INDEPENDENT THAT TELEPHONE INSTRUMENTS AND OTHER EQUIPMENT BEGAN TO BE MANUFACTURED IN INDIA AT INDIAN TELEPHONE INDUSTRIES, BANGALORE.

IT IS NOW A MASSIVE INDUSTRIAL COMPLEX WITH OVER 25,000 EMPLOYEES WORKING IN FACTORIES IN BANGALORE, NAINI, SRINAGAR, RAE BARELI AND PALGHAT.

We are grateful to Indian Telephone Industries, Bangalore for providing us with pictorial references
—Editor

ANWAR

by
Appaswami

Illustrations: V. B. Halbe

ANWAR HAS BEEN VERY NAUGHTY.

HE BROKE A GLASS THIS MORNING.

YOU MUST TALK TO HIM.

I WILL. BUT GET ME SOME TEA, FIRST.

BE VERY STRICT.

ANWAR!

GIVE ME THAT BAT.

WHY?

DO YOU WANT TO PLAY?

EH...

214

215

216

THE AMAZON-I

Script: Vaijayanti Wagle
Illustrations: Ajit Vasaikar

IN THE YEAR 1500, THE SPANISH CAPTAIN VINCENT YANEZ PINZON WAS EXPLORING THE EAST COAST OF SOUTH AMERICA SUDDENLY—

AHOY, CAPTAIN! WE ARE SAILING THROUGH FRESH WATER.

WHY THAT'S IMPOSSIBLE WE ARE 120 MILES OUT AT SEA.

A BUCKET WAS LOWERED TO SAMPLE THE WATER.

STRANGE! THIS IS INDEED FRESH WATER.

TURN THE SHIP AROUND. WE MUST UNRAVEL THIS MYSTERY.

AS THE SHIP CHANGED ITS COURSE, PINZON AND HIS CREW FOUND THEMSELVES SURROUNDED BY FRESH WATER OVER AN AREA OF 64 KM.

AMAZING! THIS MUST BE A FRESH-WATER SEA. I WILL CALL IT 'LA MER DULCE'.

BUT AS THEY EXPLORED FURTHER—

BY THE GOD ALMIGHTY, THIS IS NOT A SEA AT ALL. WE ARE IN THE MIDST OF A GIGANTIC RIVER.

WHAT HE WAS NEVER TO KNOW WAS THAT HE HAD DISCOVERED ONLY A SMALL PART OF THE AMAZON, THE WORLD'S LARGEST RIVER.

STRANGELY ENOUGH THIS MIGHTY RIVER BEGINS AS A SMALL BROOK 5600 M. HIGH IN THE SNOW-CAPPED ANDES MOUNTAINS OF PERU. FROM HERE IT PLUNGES DOWN RAVINES AND GORGES AND FLOWS THROUGH COLUMBIA AND BRAZIL TO EMPTY ITSELF OUT IN THE ATLANTIC OCEAN, 6400 KM. AWAY.

ALONG THE WAY THE MAIN TRUNK OF THE RIVER IS JOINED BY 1,100 TRIBUTARIES.

ALL THE WATER THE AMAZON AND ITS TRIBUTARIES HAVE COLLECTED POURS OUT INTO THE ATLANTIC OCEAN. THE WATER POURED OUT INTO THE OCEAN AMOUNTS TO ONE-FIFTH OF ALL THE RIVER WATERS ON EARTH.

SO GREAT IS THE TORRENT OF WATER THAT FLOWS OUT INTO THE ATLANTIC THAT IT PUSHES BACK THE SALT WATER OF THE OCEAN OVER 160 KM., WHICH IS WHY PINZON AND HIS CREW THOUGHT THEY HAD SAILED INTO A FRESH-WATER SEA.

WHERE DOES ALL THIS WATER COME FROM? SOME OF IT COMES FROM THE MELTING SNOWS OF THE ANDES MOUNTAINS.

MUCH OF THE WATER IN THE RIVER AND ITS TRIBUTARIES IS COLLECTED FROM THE RAIN THAT FALLS HERE. AND IT IS ALWAYS RAINING HERE.

IT IS EXTREMELY HOT IN THE AMAZON BASIN. THE INTENSE HEAT CAUSES WATER TO EVAPORATE. THE RESULTING WATER VAPOUR RISES HIGH AND AS IT REACHES THE COOL LAYERS ABOVE, IT FORMS BIG RAIN CLOUDS.

EVERY AFTERNOON, THE SKY DARKENS WITH THICK CLOUDS, LIGHTNING CRACKLES THROUGH THE SKY AND THE THUNDER ROLLS. SOON THE RAIN POURS DOWN IN GREAT SHEETS OF WATER.

THE AMAZON, ITS TRIBUTARIES AND THE JUNGLES AROUND THEM, COMPRISE A HUGE WILDERNESS SPREAD OUT OVER NINE SOUTH AMERICAN COUNTRIES.

AMAZON-II

Script : Vaijayanti Wagle
Illustrations : Ajit Vasaikar

THE AMAZON RIVER FLOWS THROUGH VERY THICK JUNGLE. IT IS SO DARK AND FORBIDDING THAT IT IS ALMOST UNTOUCHED BY MAN. STRANGE INSECTS, BIRDS, ANIMALS AND PLANTS ARE FOUND HERE.

THERE IS THE CANNONBALL TREE. ITS FRUIT IS AS HARD AS IRON AND WHEN IT FALLS TO THE GROUND IT MAKES A VERY LOUD SOUND.

THE AMAZONIAN VICTORIA LILY HAS HUGE LEAVES THAT LOOK LIKE GIANT-SIZED PLATES.

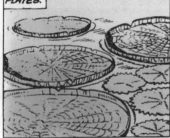

THE ANACONDA IS THE LARGEST SNAKE IN THE WORLD, OFTEN GROWING TO OVER 10 METRES. IT WRAPS ITSELF ROUND ITS VICTIM, SUFFOCATING IT AND THEN SWALLOWS IT WHOLE.

THERE ARE A WIDE VARIETY OF MONKEYS, HAPPILY JUMPING FROM TREE TO TREE.

A WOOLLY MONKEY

THE NOCTURNAL DOUROUCOOLIS

A HOWLER MONKEY

THE CAPYBARAS IS THE WORLD'S LARGEST RODENT, ALTHOUGH IT LOOKS LIKE A FIRST COUSIN OF THE PIG'S. IT CAN GROW UPTO 1¼ METRES AND WEIGHS ABOUT 73 KGS. IT HAS WEBBED FEET AND IS A VERY GOOD SWIMMER.

BECAUSE OF THE THICK VEGETATION VERY LARGE ANIMALS ARE RARE. SO IT IS THE INSECTS THAT RULE THE JUNGLE. ANTS CROWD INTO EVERY AVAILABLE SPACE. FIRE ANTS EAT EVERYTHING IN SIGHT. LEAF-EATING SAUNA ANTS CAN DESTROY GARDENS OVERNIGHT.

AND CARNIVOROUS ARMY ANTS CAN TURN A CADAVER INTO A SKELETON WITHIN MINUTES.

THE BIRD-EATING SPIDER HAS A 17½ CM. LEG SPAN. IT RUNS AND POUNCES ON ITS PREY. ITS BITE IS FATAL TO SMALL BIRDS AND INSECTS.

THOUSANDS OF SPECIES OF BUTTERFLIES FLIT THROUGH THE GLOOMY JUNGLE IN THEIR GLITTERING COLOURS.

THE RIVER WATERS ARE TEEMING WITH OVER 1500 VARIETIES OF FISH. THE DEADLY PIRANHA ARE TINY FISH THAT TRAVEL IN LARGE SCHOOLS. THEY CAN EAT A MAN OR ANIMAL TO THE BONE IN A MATTER OF MINUTES.

AND THE AMAZON BASIN IS THE HOME OF MORE THAN HALF OF THE 8,600 SPECIES OF THE BIRDS IN THE WORLD.

HUMMING BIRD

MACAW

SCARLET IBIS

TOUCAN

HOATZIN

THE CLEVER COURT JESTER

Illustrations: V. B. Halbe

Readers' Choice

Based on a story sent by N. R. Shripathi, New Mangalore

ONE DAY A SCHOLAR FROM ANOTHER COUNTRY CAME TO THE COURT OF A KING.

I CHALLENGE ANYONE HERE TO DEFEAT ME IN A BATTLE OF WITS!

A BATTLE OF WITS? I...UH... AM SURE WE CAN FIND SOMEONE TO TAKE UP YOUR CHALLENGE.

IF ANYONE DEFEATS YOU, YOU WILL PRESENT HIM WITH THIS NECKLACE. IF NOT, YOU WILL KEEP IT FOR YOURSELF.

BUT NO ONE AT THE COURT COULD DEFEAT THE MAN. AND FINALLY—

MY FRIEND, IT LOOKS AS IF YOU'VE WON!

BUT A VOICE RANG OUT—

NO! I WOULD LIKE A CHANCE AS WELL!

IT WAS THE KING'S JESTER.

NOW, I WILL ASK YOU FIVE QUESTIONS, TO ALL OF WHICH YOU MUST GIVE ME AN INCORRECT ANSWER...

223

224

225

MEET THE COW

Script: Ashvin
Illustrations : Ajit Vasaikar

CATTLE HAVE BEEN DOMESTICATED FOR THOUSANDS OF YEARS. COWS HAVE BEEN REARED FOR THEIR MILK AND THE MALES (BULLS OR OXEN) HAVE BEEN USED TO PULL HEAVY LOADS.

IND AN COWS HAVE A HUMP AND A LARGE DEWLAP.
THE DEWLAP IS THE FOLD OF SKIN HANGING DOWN FROM THEIR NECKS. THE COW LOSES EXCESS HEAT IN ITS BODY THROUGH THE DEWLAP.

A COW STARTS GIVING MILK ONLY WHEN IT HAS GIVEN BIRTH TO A CALF. AND THEN IT CONTINUES TO GIVE MILK FOR NINE TO TEN MONTHS AFTERWARDS. INDIAN COWS GIVE FIVE TO SIX LITRES OF MILK A DAY.

EUROPEAN BREEDS GIVE UPTO FIFTY LITRES OF MILK A DAY. THESE COWS ARE RAISED ESPECIALLY FOR THEIR MILK.

IF YOU LOOK AT A JERSEY COW, FOR EXAMPLE, YOU'LL SEE THAT HER UDDERS ARE SO LARGE THAT SHE CAN HARDLY WALK. JERSEY COWS, HOWEVER, PRODUCE THE RICHEST MILK.

COWS BEING MILKED BY MACHINE AT A DAIRY FARM IN EUROPE

THE PROTEIN CONTENT OF MILK IS HIGHEST FOR GUERNSEY COWS (3.91 PERCENT).

THE MILK IS PRODUCED BY THE COW FROM HER BLOOD.
EACH TIME BLOOD PASSES THROUGH THE UDDER, SOME PART OF THE BLOOD IS CHANGED INTO MILK. ABOUT 200 LITRES OF BLOOD MUST PASS THROUGH THE UDDER TO MAKE ABOUT 450 GMS. OF MILK.

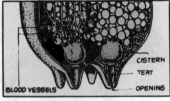

BLOOD VESSELS

CISTERN

TEAT

OPENING

SO IF A COW IS TO GIVE A LOT OF MILK, IT MUST GET A LOT OF FOOD. IN INDIA, THE COW IS FED GRAINS, BRAN AND OILCAKES IN ADDITION TO GRASS AND HAY.

EUROPE, THE U.S.A., NEW ZEALAND AND AUSTRALIA HAVE RICH GRASSLANDS AND A CLIMATE IN WHICH COWS THRIVE.
SO THEY ARE THE LARGEST MILK-PRODUCING COUNTRIES.

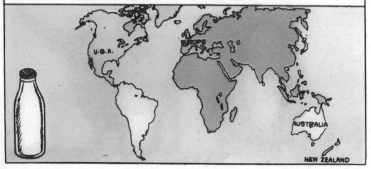

U.S.A.

EUROPE

AUSTRALIA

NEW ZEALAND

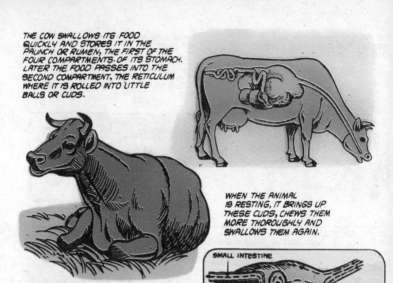

THE COW SWALLOWS ITS FOOD QUICKLY AND STORES IT IN THE PAUNCH OR RUMEN, THE FIRST OF THE FOUR COMPARTMENTS OF ITS STOMACH. LATER THE FOOD PASSES INTO THE SECOND COMPARTMENT, THE RETICULUM WHERE IT IS ROLLED INTO LITTLE BALLS OR CUDS.

WHEN THE ANIMAL IS RESTING, IT BRINGS UP THESE CUDS, CHEWS THEM MORE THOROUGHLY AND SWALLOWS THEM AGAIN.

THIS TIME THE FOOD PASSES INTO THE THIRD AND THEN INTO THE FOURTH COMPARTMENTS - THE OMASUM AND THE ABOMASUM.
DIGESTION TAKES PLACE IN THE ABOMASUM.

SMALL INTESTINE

RETICULUM
OMASUM
RUMEN
ABOMASUM

SOME EUROPEAN CATTLE LIKE THE HEREFORD COW SHOWN HERE, ARE RAISED FOR THEIR MEAT.
THESE CATTLE HAVE HEAVY WELL-ROUNDED BODIES.

WATUSSI CATTLE, BRED IN UGANDA, HAVE THE LARGEST HORNS OF ALL DOMESTIC CATTLE.

The Wonder of Wonders

A Folktale from Bihar

Script
Meera Ugra

Illustrations:
Ram Waeerkar

PERHAPS POORAN PANDE WILL KNOW.

AND BE ABLE TO GET IT FOR US, TOO.

WELL, POORAN! WHAT DO YOU THINK? CAN YOU GET THE WONDER OF WONDERS — WHATEVER IT IS?

YES, MAHARAJ. BUT YOU MUST ALLOW ME ONE MONTH...

ANOTHER PLOT TO OUTWIT ME... HMM.

...AND I WILL NEED SOME MONEY, TOO.

OF COURSE, POORAN.

A MONTH LATER, POORAN WENT TO THE MINISTER'S HOUSE.

WELCOME! WELCOME! HAVE YOU BEEN SUCCESSFUL, POORAN?

I HAVE, SIR. BUT I NEED YOUR HELP

PLEASE COME TO MY HOUSE AND TELL ME IF IT'S THE CREATURE WHICH THE GODDESS DESIRED.

I'LL COME, POORAN.

THE TWO SET OFF.

I'LL GO AND SAY IT'S THE WRONG CREATURE ...THE KING WILL BE FURIOUS! HEE HEE HEE!

I DO HOPE IT'S THE RIGHT THING...

230

231

232

WH... WHAT IS HAPPENING?

...AND MORE COTTON—

Ouiiee!!

CLANG!

POORAN! OPEN THE DOOR!

BANG! BANG!

IN A SHORT WHILE, SIR!

POORAN RUSHED TO THE COURT.

POORAN! YOU? AND WHERE IS THE WONDER OF WONDERS?

AT HOME, MAHARAJ...

...THE CREATURE IS SO ANGRY AT THE MOMENT, IT'S DIFFICULT TO CONTROL IT. PLEASE COME TO MY HOUSE TO SEE IT.

WELL... I'LL COME. BUT WHERE IS THE MINISTER?

HE HASN'T COME TODAY, MAHARAJ.

WHAT A PITY! HE'LL MISS A RARE SIGHT. LET'S GO.

THE KING WAS AMUSED WITH HIS STORY AND REWARDED POORAN PANDE HANDSOMELY. AND THE JEALOUS COURTIERS NEVER TROUBLED HIM AGAIN.

WEATHER AND CLIMATE

Script : J.D. Isloor

Illustrations :
Anand Mande

IF A FOREIGNER WERE ASKED ABOUT THE CLIMATE OF OUR COUNTRY, HE WOULD SAY IT IS WARM, AND HE WOULD BE RIGHT. BECAUSE EVEN THOUGH THE WEATHER HERE CAN BE COLD DURING WINTER AND DAMP DURING THE MONSOONS, THE GREATER PART OF INDIA IS GENERALLY WARM THROUGHOUT THE YEAR.
THE CLIMATE OF ANY COUNTRY IS THE GENERAL WEATHER OF THAT COUNTRY.

THE CLIMATE OF A PLACE HAS A GREAT DEAL TO DO WITH HOW THE PEOPLE OF THE REGION LIVE. WHAT THEY EAT AND WHAT THEY WEAR DEPEND PARTLY ON THE CLIMATE.

IN INDIA WE WEAR LIGHT COTTON CLOTHES. OUR FOOD IS MAINLY VEGETARIAN. AND OUR HOUSES ARE WELL VENTILATED.

EUROPEANS LIVE DIFFERENTLY.
THE SUN SHINES MILDLY ON THEIR COUNTRIES.
AND THE WINTERS ARE LONG. SO THEIR
HOUSES HAVE TO BE ARTIFICIALLY HEATED.
AND THEIR CLOTHING IS HEAVY AND WARM.
MEAT IS AN IMPORTANT PART OF THEIR DIET.

ESKIMOS LIVE IN A STILL COLDER CLIMATE.
THEIR HOUSES (IGLOOS) ARE BUILT OUT
OF SNOW. AS CROPS CANNOT GROW ON
THEIR LAND, THE ESKIMOS LIVE MAINLY
ON FOOD FROM THE SEA, INCLUDING FISH
AND SEALS. THEIR CLOTHING IS MADE OUT
OF ANIMAL SKINS.

THE CHIEF FACTOR IN CLIMATE IS THE
AMOUNT OF HEAT RECEIVED FROM THE
SUN. THE EARTH IS SURROUNDED BY THE
LAYER OF GAS THAT WE BREATHE AND
WHICH WE CALL THE ATMOSPHERE. BEFORE
SUNLIGHT REACHES THE SURFACE OF THE
EARTH, IT HAS TO PASS THROUGH THE
ATMOSPHERE WHICH REFLECTS ABOUT HALF
THE HEAT BACK INTO SPACE.

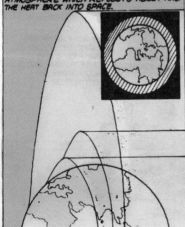

BECAUSE OF THE CURVATURE OF THE EARTH,
THE RAYS OF THE SUN HIT THE EARTH AT
DIFFERENT ANGLES.
THE RAYS ARE DIRECT AT THE EQUATOR.
SO THIS IS THE HOTTEST REGION. AT THE
POLES A SIMILAR AMOUNT OF RAYS
SPREAD OVER A LARGER DISTANCE. SO
THIS REGION RECEIVES MUCH LESS HEAT.

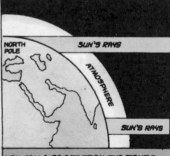

YOU CAN ALSO SEE FROM THE FIGURE
THAT THE SUN'S RAYS TRAVEL A GREATER
DISTANCE THROUGH THE ATMOSPHERE
AT THE POLAR REGION THAN AT THE
EQUATOR. BECAUSE OF THIS, THE RAYS
LOSE A LOT OF HEAT BEFORE THEY
REACH THE GROUND AT THE POLES.

OCEANS ALSO CONTRIBUTE TO THE CLIMATE OF A PLACE. LAND HEATS UP FASTER THAN WATER. LAND COOLS FASTER TOO. LONG AFTER THE LAND HAS COOLED THE WATER IS STILL VERY WARM. THIS IS WHY, IN WINTER, PLACES NEAR THE SEA, LIKE BOMBAY AND GOA ARE MUCH WARMER THAN PLACES IN THE INTERIOR LIKE NAGPUR AND AHMEDABAD.

IN SUMMER, THE HOT SUN QUICKLY HEATS UP THE LAND BUT THE WATER OF THE OCEAN TAKES TIME TO GET HEATED. AS A RESULT THE SEA IS COOLER THAN THE LAND AND PLACES NEAR THE SEA ARE COOLER THAN PLACES IN THE INTERIOR.

ALTITUDE ALSO AFFECTS CLIMATE. THE AIR IS THINNER AT HIGHER ALTITUDES AND THE TEMPERATURE DROPS ABOUT ½ °C FOR EVERY 92 METRES UP.
MOUNT CHIMBORAZO IN ECUADOR, IN SOUTH AMERICA IS ON THE EQUATOR, BUT IT HAS A PERMANENT CAP OF SNOW.

Readers choice

THE ADVENTURES OF

SUPPANDI-7

Illustrations:
Ram Waeerkar

Based on a story sent by Samiulla Sharif, Bombay

SUPPANDI! HEAT SOME WATER FOR MY BATH.

YES, SIR.

BUT... DO YOU KNOW HOW TO DO IT?

OH YES, SIR. THERE'S NOTHING SIMPLER.

...GET THE WATER...

...AND...

WHAT A QUESTION TO ASK! DOES HE THINK I'M A NITWIT!

ALL YOU HAVE TO DO IS LIGHT A FIRE...

SPLASH

!? HISSSS HISSSS

A TALE FROM GOA

Illustrations:
Ram Waeerkar

Based on a story sent by Renuka Dennis, Goa

SANTAN, A FARMER, AND HIS SON, MIGUEL WERE GOING TO A DISTANT VILLAGE.

NIGHT FELL AS THEY WERE PASSING THROUGH A FOREST.

LET US FIND A PLACE TO SLEEP.

THIS IS A GOOD SPOT.

SOMETIME LATER—

I DON'T LIKE SLEEPING ON THIS SIDE OF YOU.

COME TO THIS SIDE, THEN.

FATHER, I DON'T LIKE THIS SIDE EITHER. I WANT TO SLEEP IN THE MIDDLE.

MIDDLE?

240

OH, ALL RIGHT...

WAGH, THE TIGER WAS ON THE PROWL.

I CAN SMELL A MAN.

AH, HERE HE IS.

BUT I SEE FOUR LEGS. MAN HAS TWO.

WHAT STRANGE CREATURE IS THIS? I WILL ASK MANGEM, THE CROCODILE!

242

243

PRINCE ABHAYA

Story:
Motilal Surana

Illustrations:
Ram Waeerkar

PRINCE ABHAYA WAS ON A VISIT TO HIS UNCLE, THE KING OF SUMERPUR. THE KING WAS A LOVER OF SPORT...

...AND YOUR ARROW MUST PIERCE THE EYE OF THAT CLAY BIRD.

THE FIRST ARCHER MISSED...

...SO DID THE SECOND...

...AND THE REST OF THEM.

MAY I DISPLAY MY SKILL, UNCLE?

WHY NOT, ABHAYA.

ABHAYA STRUNG THE BOW...

...AND —

SNICK

THAT WAS GREAT ABHAYA, MY BOY.

O, THANK YOU, UNCLE.

THE CHILDLESS KING WAS FULL OF JOY.

244

THAT NIGHT —

I WISH I HAD A SON LIKE ABHAYA — HE'S SO SKILLED.

WHY DON'T WE ADOPT HIM, THEN?

YES, BUT I MUST TEST HIM FURTHER.

THE NEXT DAY —

OH, OH!

WE'LL GET IT OUT IMMEDIATELY, UNCLE.

THE KING'S RING HAD SLIPPED AND FALLEN INTO A DITCH.

WAIT A MINUTE, ABHAYA, CAN YOU TAKE THAT RING OUT WITHOUT ENTERING THAT DITCH?

HMM! GIVE ME A FEW DAYS, UNCLE.

TAKE AS MUCH TIME AS YOU LIKE.

245

NOW, BREAK THE CAKE.

HERE, UNCLE — YOUR RING.

GOOD BOY, ABHAYA.

BUT YOU HAVE ONE MORE TEST COMING UP, SON.

JUST THEN —

SALUTATIONS, MAHARAJ, PRINCE ABHAYA!

WHAT DO YOU WANT?

I'VE COME TO GET MY EYE BACK, PRINCE. HERE'S THE MONEY.

Y—YOUR EYE?

248

249

250

THIS HAPPENED TO ME ...

One evening I was returning home from college on my bicycle. It was a pleasant evening and I was feeling on top of the world. The road was somewhat deserted so I left the handlebars and road merrily in the middle of the road.

Suddenly there was a screech of brakes and a police jeep stopped behind me. Sitting inside was the Superintendent of Police himself. He asked me to accompany him. My bike and I were taken to the police station.

We got down in front of the police station, but instead of going in, the S.P. gave some orders to a constable, pointing towards a bicycle-repair shop nearby.

Five minutes later, the S.P. turned to me and said, "Here son, take your bike. And since you don't need the handlebars, we'll keep them with us at the police station!"

The bicycle was returned to me minus the handlebars!

● This true life story has been sent by Suvidhi Surana of Yeotmal.

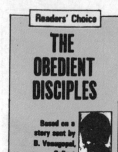

Readers' Choice

THE OBEDIENT DISCIPLES

Based on a story sent by B. Venugopal, Calicut

Illustrations: S.N. Sawant

ONCE UPON A TIME, THERE LIVED A SAGE WHO HAD MANY YOUNG DISCIPLES.

THE SAGE WAS RATHER VAIN.

FOLD YOUR HANDS WHENEVER YOU SEE ME.

ONE DAY THE SAGE AND HIS DISCIPLES WENT FOR A WALK.

SUDDENLY —

253

ANWAR

by
Appaswami

Illustrations: V. B. Halbe

254

THE FOOLISH WEAVER

Script: Gayatri Madan Dutt
Illustrations: V.B Halbe

THERE WAS ONCE A WEAVER WHO WAS FOND OF SHOWING OFF. ONE DAY, AS HE WAS PREPARING TO LEAVE FOR HIS FATHER-IN-LAW'S VILLAGE, A THOUGHT STRUCK HIM.

IF I LOOKED RICH AND IMPRESSIVE, EVERYONE WOULD ENVY MY FATHER-IN-LAW FOR HAVING GOT HOLD OF SUCH A FINE SON-IN-LAW!

AND SO—

FRIEND, COULD I BORROW YOUR MARE FOR A FEW DAYS?

WELL... ALL RIGHT. BUT DO TAKE CARE OF IT.

FRIEND, COULD I BORROW YOUR JEWELS AND CLOTHES FOR A WHILE?

ALL RIGHT— BUT BE CAREFUL WITH THEM.

SOON—

HE, HE, HE! EVERYONE'S GAZING AT ME WITH SUCH ADMIRATION!

SUDDENLY, ON THE WAY —

OH, NO — A STORM!

RUMBLE

I WILL HAVE TO WAIT AT THIS VILLAGE TILL IT CLEARS. WHAT A NUISANCE!

THE STORM RAGED FOR A LONG TIME. IT WAS LATE EVENING BY THE TIME THE WEAVER COULD CONTINUE HIS JOURNEY.

HERE'S FATHER-IN-LAW'S VILLAGE AT LAST, AND NOT A SOUL ABOUT!

IF I ENTER NOW, NOBODY WILL SEE ME ALL DRESSED UP. I'D RATHER MAKE A GRAND ENTRANCE IN THE MORNING.

SEEING A HUT NEARBY, THE WEAVER WENT UP TO IT.

ANYBODY IN?

KNOCK KNOCK

WHAT DO YOU WANT?

GREETINGS, GOOD FAKIR. I AM JUST A TRAVELLER WANTING SHELTER FOR THE NIGHT.

257

SO, DRESSED IN THE FAKIR'S TATTERS, THE WEAVER SET OUT.

SEEK ALMS AT EVERY HOUSE. I HAVE TAKEN A VOW TO HONOUR EVERY HOUSE BY EATING WHAT EACH OFFERS.

I CAN RECOGNISE THE FOOD FROM EVERY HOUSE, SO BE SURE TO DO AS I SAY.

THEN I'LL HAVE TO GO TO MY FATHER-IN-LAW'S HOUSE ALSO!

SOON THE WEAVER ARRIVED AT HIS FATHER-IN-LAW'S.

OH, THE GRAIN PIT! IT'S FULL OF WATER FROM THIS MORNING'S STORM.

ALMS! ALMS FOR A FAKIR.

I'M COMING, SIR.

HELP! IT'S MY WIFE. SHE MUSN'T RECOGNISE ME...

...AAA...

...HAAH!

EEEE! FATHER, MOTHER— A FAKIR'S FALLEN INTO THE PIT!

NEIGHBOURS, NEIGHBOURS COME! SOMETHING'S HAPPENED NEXT DOOR.

WHAT IS IT?

GET A LIGHT SOMEONE.

258

259

A TAIL'S TALE
Illustrations: Ashok Dongre

Readers' Choice — Based on a story sent by Rashmi Mishra, Khagadia, Bihar

ONE EVENING, IN SHEIKH INHAAM IBN MOOSA'S DESERT CAMP—

UNCLE! THE GOLD COINS HAVE BEEN STOLEN!

WHAT?

IT WAS BAAKAR, THE SHEIKH'S NEPHEW.

THE THIEF HAS GOT TO BE SOMEONE IN MY CAMP.

TELL THE MEN WHAT HAS HAPPENED AND SUMMON THEM AT ONCE, BAAKAR.

Y-YES, UNCLE.

WHEN THE MEN ASSEMBLED—

THIS MAGIC DONKEY WILL REVEAL THE THIEF TO ME.

HE LED THE DONKEY INTO A TENT.

EACH ONE OF YOU WILL GO IN AND HOLD THE DONKEY'S TAIL — THE DONKEY WILL BLURT OUT THE THIEF'S NAME WHEN THE THIEF HOLDS IT.

GO IN NOW... ONE BY ONE.

261

262

Ⓓ THE MOVING ARROW

You will need : A glass, water, a piece of card.

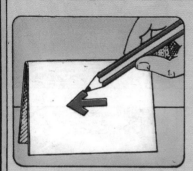

1 Fold a sheet of card in half and draw an arrow in the centre of one side.

2. Stand the card on a table and place an empty glass in front of the card. Now, can you change the direction of the arrow without touching the card ?

3. You can do so just by filling the glass with water !

THE THIEF IN THE TUB

Romantic Tales of the Punjab

Script: Anju Aggarwal
Illustrations:
Ram Waeerkar

ONE DAY, A LITTLE BOY WAS PLAYING OUTSIDE HIS HOUSE. HE HAPPENED TO LOOK INTO A TUB OF WATER AND SAW HIS REFLECTION IN IT.

OH!

MOTHER, MOTHER!

MOTHER! THERE IS A CHILD IN THIS TUB...

... BEGGING FOR BREAD.

HUSBAND! COME HERE!

LOOK INTO THE TUB AND SEE IF ANYONE IS THERE.

WIFE, THERE IS NO CHILD HERE, BUT...

... AN OLD VILLAIN, A THIEF.

GET INTO THE HOUSE QUICKLY.

THE MAN PICKED UP A STONE...

...AND HURLED IT INTO THE TUB.

?

THERE'S NO ONE HERE.

CUNNING RASCAL— THAT THIEF...

... I DON'T KNOW HOW HE ESCAPED. BUT HE IS NOT LIKELY TO TROUBLE US AGAIN.

Kalia
THE CROW

Script:
PRASAD
Illustrations:
ASHOK DONGRE

THE FOREST IS CERTAINLY THICK HERE, CHAMATAKA.

HEH! HEH! THAT GIVES ME AN IDEA.

WHAT ARE THOSE TWO UP TO?

TIE THAT VINE TO THOSE TREES, DOOB DOOB. I'LL HIDE FURTHER UP THE TRACK...

... AND SEE IF I CAN DRIVE A DEER OR SOMETHING TOWARDS THIS PLACE.

WHEN I SHOUT "NOW!", LIFT THE VINE, SO THAT THE ANIMAL TRIPS.

WHAT A CLEVER IDEA, CHAMATAKA!

YES, VERY CLEVER! IT MIGHT EVEN WORK IF I DON'T DO SOMETHING ABOUT IT.

266

267

FORTUNE HELPS THOSE WHO HELP THEMSELVES

Script: Toni Patel
Illustrations: Ram Waeerkar

THE COURT OF RAJA KETAN ATTRACTED TALENTED YOUNG MEN FROM THE ENTIRE COUNTRY WHO HOPED TO GET EMPLOYMENT IN HIS SERVICE. MADHO PRASAD WAS ONE SUCH. LIKE THE OTHERS, HE TOO HURRIED TO DO THE KING LITTLE SERVICES...

...OR LAUGHED AS LOUDLY AS THE REST AT THE KING'S SMALLEST JOKES.

HA! HA! HA!

BUT THE KING DID NOT GIVE HIM ANY WORK.

ONE DAY, A BAKER OFFERED HIM A JOB AND MADHO PRASAD ACCEPTED IT.

SO ALL DAY HE WOULD SIT AT THE BAKER'S GRINDING CORN...

...AND IN THE EVENING HE WOULD ATTEND THE KING'S COURT AS USUAL.

WHO KNOWS? FORTUNE MAY STILL SMILE ON ME SOMEDAY!

ONE DAY, AS THE KING WAS DRIVING OUT IN HIS CHARIOT, HE HAPPENED TO PASS THE BAKERY.

CAN IT REALLY BE MADHO PRASAD?

WHAT ON EARTH IS HE WORKING THERE FOR?

THE KING'S CURIOSITY WAS AROUSED...

...AND THE MOMENT MADHO PRASAD CAME TO THE COURT THAT EVENING...

THE KING RAISED HIS EYEBROWS QUESTIONINGLY AT HIM AND CLOSING HIS RIGHT FIST...

...SLOWLY TURNED IT ROUND AND ROUND, AS IF HE WERE GRINDING WHEAT.

MADHO PRASAD WAS VERY EMBARRASSED.

IF THESE PEOPLE COME TO KNOW I'M WORKING FOR A BAKER, THEY'LL LAUGH ME OUT OF COURT.

HE TOO, DECIDED TO USE MIME TO REPLY.

MY STOMACH...

...HAS FORCED ME TO WORK WITH BOTH MY HANDS,...

...TO EARN TWO ANNAS.

THE KING UNDERSTOOD HIM PERFECTLY.

AH! POOR FELLOW! I MUST DO SOMETHING TO HELP HIM!

BUT THE MIMED DIALOGUE HAD A STRANGE EFFECT ON THE COURTIERS.

WHAT WERE THE KING AND MADHO PRASAD SAYING TO EACH OTHER?

THAT'S WHAT WE MUST FIND OUT.

YES. MADHO PRASAD COULD BE A SPY.

SO FROM THE NEXT DAY ONWARDS—

O MADHO PRASAD, DO HAVE A PAAN!

NO, NO HAVE ONE OF MINE!

O MADHO PRASAD, DO LOOK AT THIS TINY PERFUME BOTTLE! IT'S JUST ARRIVED FROM LUCKNOW. DO ACCEPT IT FROM ME!

BUT FINALLY, ONE OF THEM DARED ASK THE QUESTION THAT WAS UPPERMOST IN ALL THEIR MINDS.

O MADHO PRASAD, COME, COME, NOW. DO TELL US, HA! HA! I MEAN, WHAT WERE YOU SAYING IN ONE OF THOSE SECRET SIGN CONVERSATIONS YOU WERE HAVING WITH THE KING!

ALL THESE RASCALS HAVE BEEN ROBBING THE KING IN ONE WAY OR THE OTHER...

...AND NOW THEY'RE AFRAID I MIGHT HAVE FOUND THEM OUT.

THIS IS MY CHANCE TO MAKE SOME MONEY.

WELL YOU SEE, BY CLOSING HIS RIGHT HAND, THE KING WARNED ME NOT TO DISCLOSE ROYAL SECRETS TO ANY ONE...

...AND BY THE CIRCULAR MOVEMENT OF HIS HAND, HE WAS ENQUIRING IF I HAD TOURED THE TOWN ON INSPECTION, AS HE HAD ORDERED.

OF COURSE, I BY MY GESTURES, IN RETURN ASSURED THE KING THAT HIS SECRETS WERE SAFE WITH ME...

...THAT NOT ONE OF THESE SECRETS WOULD ESCAPE FROM ME...

...AND THAT IN TWO DAYS TIME I WOULD HAVE PROOF OF ALL I HAD DISCOVERED, TO PLACE BEFORE THE KING.

WHAT ARE WE TO DO? WE ARE LOST IF THE KING LEARNS OF OUR ACTIVITIES.

WHAT SHALL WE DO? WELL, WE CAN SILENCE HIM FOR-EVER. TIE A STONE ROUND HIS NECK AND DROWN HIM IN THE RIVER.

YES! YES! GET RID OF THE RASCAL!

BUT WHEN HE DISAPPEARS THE KING WILL KNOW AT ONCE WE DID IT!

AND WE'LL BE IN GREATER TROUBLE THAN EVER!

OF COURSE! WHY DIDN'T WE THINK OF IT BEFORE? GIVE HIM A LARGE SUM OF MONEY TO KEEP HIM QUIET!

EACH ONE CONTRIBUTED GENEROUSLY—

AND A HEAVY PURSE FILLED WITH GOLD COINS WAS PRESENTED TO MADHO PRASAD.

ACCEPT THIS, MADHO PRASAD AS A TOKEN OF OUR RESPECT!

MADHO PRASAD, NOW A RICH MAN, GOT HIMSELF A BEAUTIFUL HOUSE AND WENT EVERY-WHERE IN AN OPEN PALANQUIN.

PRETTY SOON, THE KING WHO WAS OUT ON ONE OF HIS INSPECTIONS, CAME ACROSS MADHO PRASAD ON HIS PALANQUIN.

WHO HAVE WE HERE? IT'S MADHO PRASAD!

WHAT A STRANGE MAN YOU ARE. ONE DAY I SEE YOU GRINDING CORN FOR A LIVE-LIHOOD. THE NEXT, I SEE YOU BORNE ABOUT ON A PALANQUIN. HOW DID YOU MANAGE TO BECOME RICH SO SUDDENLY?

YOUR HIGHNESS, IT WAS ALL YOUR DOING. I OWE ALL MY PRESENT PROSPERITY TO YOU.

WHEN HE HAD RELATED THE STORY IN EVERY DETAIL, THE KING SHOOK WITH LAUGHTER.

HO! HO! HO! YOU ARE A CLEVER MAN, MADHO PRASAD AND QUICK-WITTED TOO!

YOU SHALL BE MY MINISTER OF STATE. THEN MY COURTIERS WILL REALLY HAVE SOMETHING TO WORRY ABOUT!

THE REMEDY FOR BALDNESS

Story by Lalita Kodikal

Illustrations: V.B. Halbe

CLEVER STEFAN

A Serbian Folktale

Illustrations : V.B. Halbe

Based on a story sent by
D. Antony Rajesh

Readers' Choice

MAN: YEARS AGO SERBIA* WAS CONQUERED BY TURKEY.

THE LAND WAS RULED BY THE TURKISH PASHAS WHO LORDED IT OVER THE LOCAL PEASANTS. ONE SUCH WAS JEMAL PASHA—

THERE GOES JEMAL PASHA! HE'S A FAIR MAN, BUT HE IS VERY STRICT.

YES. BUT I WISH HE WOULDN'T IMPOSE SUCH HEAVY TAXES ON US.

AND I WISH HE'D STOP CONFISCATING OUR PROPERTY IF WE DON'T PAY THE TAXES ON TIME.

NOW JEMAL PASHA WAS ON A TAX-COLLECTING MISSION.

STEFAN! YOU HAVE NOT PAID YOUR TAXES. PAY UP AT ONCE, OR ELSE...

BUT, MY LORD, I DON'T HAVE THE MONEY...

I DON'T WANT TO LISTEN TO EXCUSES. I'LL JUST HAVE TO CONFISCATE YOUR HORSE.

OH, NO! PLEASE DON'T DO THAT! HE'S MY PET AND I CAN'T DO WITHOUT HIM.

* MODERN YUGOSLAVIA

278

STEFAN, I HAVE A DUTY TO PERFORM, THE HORSE NOW BELONGS TO THE TURKISH GOVERNMENT. SO STAND ASIDE.

AND JEMAL PASHA RODE AWAY LEADING STEFAN'S HORSE.

JEMAL MAY BE DUTY-BOUND... BUT THE TURKS HAVE NO RIGHT TO RULE OUR LAND AND TAKE OUR PROPERTY. BUT HOW CAN I GET BACK MY HORSE?

NOW JEMAL PASHA HAD A VERY FOOLISH WIFE. ONE DAY STEFAN CAME UPON HER SITTING ON A ROCK.

THERE'S JEMAL PASHA'S WIFE WATERING MY HORSE. I'LL HAVE A WORD WITH HER.

GOOD MORNING.

GOOD MORNING. AND WHERE DO YOU COME FROM?

FROM THE OTHER WORLD!

REALLY! AND HOW IS MY POOR SON, MUSTAFA, FARING THERE?

280

281

STOP!

HEE HEE HEE! THAT'S FOOLED HIM.

HELP! KEEP OFF!

STOP! YOU RASCAL!

WHERE'S THE BAG OF GOLD COINS?

WHAT GOLD COINS, MY LORD?

DON'T STALL ME!

MY LORD, I DON'T HAVE ANY GOLD COINS WITH ME. I'M BUT A POOR MILLER.

JEMAL PASHA SWIFTLY SEARCHED THE BAFFLED MILLER.

BUT HE COULD NOT FIND THE GOLD COINS. AT LAST IT DAWNED ON JEMAL PASHA THAT HE HAD BEEN TRICKED. HE RACED BACK.

PUFF! PUFF!

WIFE! HERE I AM... WHY, WHERE'S THE HORSE?

THAT NICE YOUNG MAN CAME BACK HERE AND RETURNED THE GOLD COINS.

OH! THAT'S GOOD. BUT WHY WOULD HE DO THAT?

YOU SEE, ACCORDING TO HIM, OUR SON HAS WON A LOTTERY AND HE HAS PLENTY OF MONEY. BUT HE WANTS A HORSE BADLY.

SO I GAVE HIM THE HORSE TO GIVE TO OUR SON.

OH, NO!

HE'S NOWHERE TO BE SEEN. THE SCOUNDREL. HE'S TRICKED US THOROUGHLY.

STEFAN RODE MERRILY AWAY TO A NEIGHBOURING COUNTRY, HAPPY AT HAVING GOT HIS HORSE BACK.

THE ADVENTURES OF SUPPANDI - 8

Readers' Choice

Illustrations
Ram Waeerkar

Based on a story sent by Sandesh Parrikar Goa

ONE MORNING —

I NEED A MATCHBOX, SUPPANDI.

I'LL GO AND BUY ONE, SIR.

ON THE WAY BACK FROM THE SHOP —

I HOPE THIS MATCHBOX IS FRESH...

...I'LL TRY A MATCHSTICK TO MAKE SURE...

... AAH! LIGHTS WELL!

THIS ONE TOO, IS ALL RIGHT.

LATER, AT HOME —

THE MATCHBOX, SUPPANDI.

HERE YOU ARE, SIR. IT'S A VERY FRESH ONE, TOO!

I TRIED ALL THE MATCHSTICKS ON THE WAY HOME!

??

Kalia THE CROW

Illustrations:
RAM WAEERKAR

I WONDER WHAT'S GOING ON THERE.

RABBITS FIGHTING.

IT'S DOOB DOOB AND CHAMATAKA!

RUN!

THEY WERE PLAYING... BUT WHAT A CROWD HAD COLLECTED AROUND THEM.

WHY DON'T WE HAVE A FIGHT TOO.

A FIGHT?

BUT WHY SHOULD WE FIGHT?

A SHAM FIGHT, YOU DOPE!

I'LL HIT YOU AND THEN YOU HIT ME... NOT TOO HARD OF COURSE.

285

MERCURY

Script: J.D. Isloor
Illustrations: Anand Mande

MERCURY IS THE PLANET CLOSEST TO THE SUN. IT IS ALSO THE SMALLEST AND FASTEST MOVING PLANET IN OUR SOLAR SYSTEM.

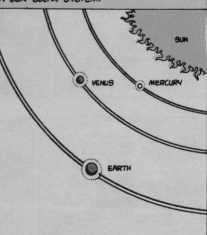

MERCURY RACES ALONG ITS ORBIT AROUND THE SUN AT THE GREAT SPEED OF 48 KM PER SECOND. THE NEXT IN THE RACE IS VENUS WITH A SPEED OF 35 KM PER SECOND. THE EARTH FOLLOWS THIRD AT 30 KM PER SECOND.

BUT MERCURY IS VERY SLOW IN TURNING ROUND ON ITS OWN AXIS. IT IS SO SLOW THAT FROM ONE SUNRISE TO THE NEXT, IT TAKES 59 EARTH DAYS.

THE ANCIENT GREEKS WHO DISCOVERED MERCURY IN 3000 B.C. KNEW THAT IT MOVED VERY FAST. THAT'S WHY THEY NAMED IT HERMES, AFTER THE SWIFT MESSENGER OF THE GODS. MERCURY IS ITS ROMAN NAME. INDIANS CALL IT BUDHA AND ASSOCIATE IT WITH INTELLIGENCE.

MERCURY IS ABOUT THE SIZE OF PLUTO, THE PLANET FARTHEST FROM THE SUN AND IS SLIGHTLY LARGER THAN OUR MOON. ITS DIAMETER IS ONLY 4880 KM. IT WOULD JUST FIT INTO THE ATLANTIC OCEAN WERE IT TO BE BROUGHT ON TO THE EARTH.

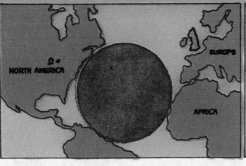

BEING CLOSEST TO THE SUN, MERCURY RECEIVES MAXIMUM HEAT AND LIGHT. THE SUN LOOKS 3 TIMES BIGGER ON MERCURY THAN IT DOES TO US ON EARTH AND SHINES FIERCELY BECAUSE MERCURY HAS NO ATMOSPHERE. ITS DAY-TIME TEMPERATURE IS AS HIGH AS 400°C. AT NIGHT THE TEMPERATURE DROPS TO −200°C

IT IS NOT EASY TO SEE MERCURY FROM THE EARTH BECAUSE OF ITS CLOSENESS TO THE SUN. THE SUN'S BRIGHTNESS DOES NOT ALLOW US TO SEE DETAILS OF ITS SURFACE.

BUT THE PLANET HAS BEEN PHOTOGRAPHED BY THE MARINER-10 SPACECRAFT WHEN IT FLEW CLOSE TO MERCURY IN 1975. THE PHOTOGRAPHS SHOW ITS SURFACE TO BE JUST LIKE OUR MOON – FULL OF CRATERS, HIGHLANDS AND PLAINS.

The word Rupee has evolved from the Sanskrit term *Raupya* which means wrought silver.

Although the date of origin of coinage in India is not certain, coins as currency began to be widely used during the Mauryan and Gupta periods. But it was Sher Shah Sur who issued coins in silver by the name of *Rupiya* and made them standard currency throughout his empire. He also issued copper *Paisas.*

Throughout the Mughal period, the Rupiya remained the standard unit of currency.

Among the Indo - Europeans, the Portuguese, who were the first to establish a mint in Goa, adopted the word *Rupia* for their coins in 1775.

When the English introduced their own coins they changed the word *Rupiya* to *Rupee*. They issued one rupee, half-rupee and quarter-rupee coins in silver.

With the advent of freedom, the rupee continued to be divided along the old pattern of quarters. But with the introduction of the decimal system on April 1, 1957 the rupee became equivalent to 100 paise.

How to whiten charcoal

Illustrations: Ram Waeerkar

Adapted from the folktale as told by the late Saguna Manjeshwar.

ONE DAY BHONDURAM FOUND A PIECE OF CHARCOAL ON THE STREET.

POOR THING! IT'S SO BLACK!

DON'T BE SAD, LITTLE ONE.

I'LL MAKE YOU WHITE.

UNCLE!

YES?

IT'S BHONDU, THE SIMPLETON.

HOW CAN I MAKE THIS CHARCOAL WHITE?

WHY! THAT'S EASY...

...WASH IT WITH MILK.

MILK, EH?

BHONDU WENT TO THE MILKMAN.

UNCLE...ER... PLEASE GIVE ME SOME MILK.

294

...AND BEGAN TO WASH THE PIECE OF COAL WITH SOAP AND WATER.

HEY, BHONDU, COME TO PLAY!

I CAN'T! I HAVE BETTER THINGS TO DO.

WHAT ARE YOU DOING?

HOW DUMB CAN YOU GET! I AM WASHING THIS CHARCOAL SO THAT IT BECOMES WHITE.

HAH! FOR THAT YOU MUST RUB IT ON A GRINDING STONE. DON'T YOU KNOW THAT, CLEVER ONE?

OH!

OF COURSE I KNOW THAT... NOW LEAVE ME ALONE.

SO BHONDU BEGAN TO RUB THE PIECE OF CHARCOAL ON A GRINDING STONE.

SOMETIME LATER—

WHAT ARE YOU DOING, SON?

I...ER...

296

MAKE YOUR OWN **LETTER HOLDER**

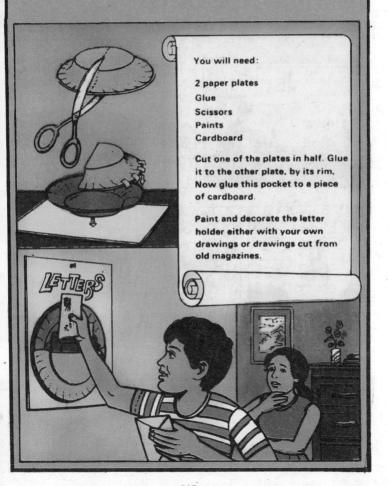

You will need:

2 paper plates
Glue
Scissors
Paints
Cardboard

Cut one of the plates in half. Glue it to the other plate, by its rim. Now glue this pocket to a piece of cardboard.

Paint and decorate the letter holder either with your own drawings or drawings cut from old magazines.

SURESH'S CAT

Illustrations: Ashok Dongre

Based on a story sent by Sanjay Colaso. Margao, Goa

TWO FROGS

Illustrations Ashok Dongre

Readers' Choice

Based on a story sent by Mirza Gasanfar Ali Baig, Hyderabad

TWO FROGS WENT TO A DAIRY.

WHEN THEY WERE INSIDE—

I WONDER WHAT ALL THESE BARRELS CONTAIN?

LET'S JUMP INTO ONE AND SEE WHAT'S IN IT.

AND SO—

SPLASH

WHAT'S THIS?

IT'S MILK.

OH DEAR, OH DEAR!

THERE'S NOTHING TO WORRY ABOUT. JUST KEEP SWIMMING AND YOU'LL BE ALL RIGHT.

THAT'S WHAT YOU THINK! I CAN'T STAND THIS SMELL! I'M GETTING OUT!

AGAIN AND AGAIN THE FROG TRIED TO CLIMB OUT OF THE BARREL.

BUT EACH TIME HE SLIPPED AND FELL...

... AND FINALLY —

GLUB GLUB GLUB GLUB

HE HAS DROWNED! MY POOR FRIEND!

THE OTHER FROG KEPT THRASHING ABOUT.

AFTER SOME TIME—

THIS MILK IS BECOMING THICKER AND THICKER...

...AND THICKER.

BY MORNING THE MILK HAD TURNED INTO BUTTER AND THE FROG JUMPED OUT OF THE BARREL, VERY TIRED, BUT SAFE.

THE RAIN-MAKER

Illustrations: S. N. Sawant

Based on a story sent by Ramesh M.K., Bombay

ONCE THERE WAS AN ASTROLOGER. EVERYBODY IN HIS VILLAGE CAME TO HIM TO HAVE THEIR FORTUNES TOLD.

AND AS HIS FEES WERE HIGH, HE MADE A LOT OF MONEY.

ONE YEAR THERE WAS A DROUGHT.

MY FIELDS ARE PARCHED.

MINE, TOO.

WHEN WILL THE RAINS COME?

IN DESPAIR, THE HEADMAN WENT TO THE ASTROLOGER.

TELL ME, WHEN WILL IT RAIN?

SOON.

GIVE US A DEFINITE DATE.

WE CAN WAIT NO LONGER.

WHAT SHOULD I DO NOW?

302

303

Kalia
THE CROW

Script:
DENIS

Illustrations:
RAM WAEERKAR

WHAT'S HAPPENED, CHAMATAKA? ARE YOU ILL?

SSHH...! DON'T DISTURB HIM. HE'S FASTING.

FASTING?

I AM REPENTING FOR ALL MY PAST SINS, KALIA.

THAT'S NICE! BUT I MUST BE OFF. BYE!

PEACE BE WITH YOU!

I'D BETTER KEEP AN EYE ON THESE TWO.

GOT RID OF HIM AT LAST.

I'M HUNGRY. TIME TO EAT SOME HONEY.

WAIT! WHAT IF SOMEBODY COMES ALONG?

TELL THEM I AM INSIDE — MEDITATING.

MEDITATION, PAAH! HE HAS RUSHED BACK TO THE HONEY COMBS HE STOLE FROM BABLOO'S CAVE.

OH! OH!

304

SUDDENLY—

THUM THUMP

GR... SOMEBODY STOLE MY HONEYCOMBS. WHERE WERE YOU LAST NIGHT?

I...I...I... HAVE GIVEN UP STEALING. I AM NOW ON A FAST...

YOU TOO CAN COME IN, BABLOO. LOTS OF HONEY IN HERE.

SO YOU ARE FASTING, HUH!

RASCAL! WILL YOU NEVER IMPROVE?

TIME FOR ME TO LEAVE.

GO— JOIN YOUR FRIEND.

SPLASH

BLUB... GLUG... AH...

HE HAS SWALLOWED A LOT OF WATER!

BROTHER CHAMATAKA HAS BROKEN HIS FAST AT LAST. HA, HA, HA!

306

Make your own **MAGIC RINGS**

You will need: A strip of paper (about 4 cm x 30 cm or longer)
Scissors
Glue

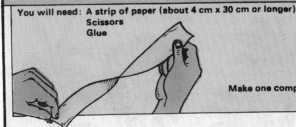

Make one complete twist.

Glue the two ends together,

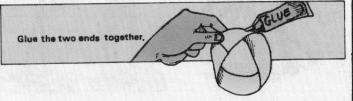

Draw a line along the centre all the way around and then cut all along the line.

The result is not two rings, as you might have supposed, but one big ring, double the size of the original ring.

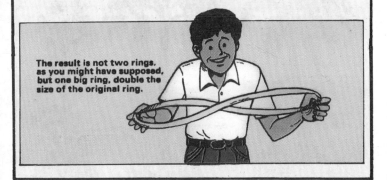

OUR PALMS

Script: J.D. Isloor ■ Illustrations: J.P. Irani

IT IS EASY TO IDENTIFY A PALM TREE. IT HAS A LONG CYLINDRICAL STEM, CROWNED WITH A TUFT OF LEAVES. AND IT HAS NO BRANCHES. THERE ARE SEVERAL TYPES OF PALMS:

COCONUT PALM

PALMYRA PALM

ARECA PALM

DATE PALM

MALABAR SAGO PALM

RATTAN CANE PALM

308

COCONUT PALM

THIS MAJESTIC PALM IS KNOWN AS 'KALPA VRIKSHA' IN HINDU MYTHOLOGY. IT MEANS 'WISH TREE' IN SANSKRIT. THE TREE IS SYMBOLIC OF LONGEVITY. ITS FRUIT, THE COCONUT IS SACRED TO HINDUS.

PEOPLE LIVING IN COASTAL AREAS, ESPECIALLY THOSE WHO DEPEND UPON THE SEA FOR THEIR LIVELIHOOD OFFER COCONUT FRUITS TO VARUNA, THE GOD OF THE SEAS. 'COCONUT DAY' IS CONSIDERED MOST SACRED FOR THIS OFFERING.

THIS PALM CAN GROW TO A HEIGHT OF 25 M. THE TRUNK IS MARKED WITH SEMI-CIRCULAR SCARS. THEY INDICATE THE PLACES WHERE NEW BOUGHS, NOW FALLEN, HAD SPROUTED. YOU CAN TELL THE AGE OF THE TREE BY COUNTING THE SCARS. TEN TO TWELVE SCARS REPRESENT ONE YEAR AS BOUGHS SPROUT AT THE RATE OF ABOUT ONE PER MONTH.

A WELL CULTIVATED TREE CAN YIELD ABOUT 300 TO 400 COCONUTS PER YEAR, BUT THE AVERAGE YIELD IN OUR COUNTRY IS MUCH LESS.

YOU WILL NOT FIND ANOTHER TREE AS USEFUL AS THE COCONUT PALM. EVERY PART OF THE TREE IS USEFUL. THE NUT, WHEN TENDER, CONTAINS DELICIOUS WATER AND SWEET FLESH. IT IS NOT ONLY THIRST-QUENCHING, BUT VERY NUTRITIOUS, TOO. IT CONTAINS SUGAR, MINERALS AND VITAMINS.

WHEN THE FRUIT IS RIPE IT IS USED IN COOKING. IT IS THE FAVOURITE INGREDIENT IN MANY FOOD PREPARATIONS OF PEOPLE LIVING IN THE COASTAL REGIONS.

THE DRIED KERNEL IS KNOWN AS 'COPRA'. THIS IS USED IN MAKING DRY CHUTNEYS AND EXTRACTING OIL. COCONUT OIL IS AN EDIBLE OIL USED NOT ONLY IN COOKING BUT ALSO IN COSMETICS, MEDICINES AND SOAP-MAKING.

PURE COCONUT OIL

AFTER THE OIL HAS BEEN EXTRACTED FROM COPRA, WHATEVER IS LEFT BEHIND ARE CALLED OIL-CAKES. THESE ARE USED AS CATTLE FEED.

THE FIBRE COVERING THE SHELL IS CALLED COIR. THE COIR IS USED IN MAKING ROPES, CARPETS, DOORMATS, MATTRESSES AND BRUSHES. THE COIR EARNS SUBSTANTIAL FOREIGN EXCHANGE FOR INDIA.

A VERY SWEET SAP CALLED 'NEERA' IS COLLECTED BY MAKING A CUT ON THE YOUNG TREE. WHEN FERMENTED, IT BECOMES 'TODDY' WHICH IS AN INTOXICATING DRINK.

BROOMS ARE MADE FROM THE LEAF-RIBS.

THE COCONUT TREE IS RIGHTLY CALLED 'GREEN GOLD.'

THE RIVER OF DIAMONDS

READERS' CHOICE

Illustrations: S.N. Sawant

Based on a story sent by
Ramandeep Bedi, Patiala.

SHYAM HAD DECIDED TO GO TO THE CITY.
AS HE WAS ABOUT TO LEAVE—

SON, I'VE NOTHING TO GIVE YOU...

...EXCEPT THIS SMALL DIAMOND.

MOTHER...I...

TAKE IT!

SO SHYAM TOOK THE DIAMOND, TUCKED IT INTO HIS DHOTI...

...BID HIS MOTHER A TEARFUL FAREWELL...

...AND SET OUT. AT NOON, AS HE WAS HALF-WAY THROUGH A JUNGLE—

ROBBERS!

HAND OVER YOUR BELONGINGS!

A-ALL RIGHT!

311

312

313

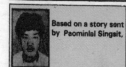

Readers' Choice
THE WEATHER FORECAST

Based on a story sent by Paominlal Singsit.

Illustrations : Anand Mande

ONCE TWO MEN WERE MOTORING IN A LONELY PART OF AMERICA—

WHAT A VAST, DESOLATE AREA!

YES, THERE'S NOT A SOUL TO BE SEEN.

BUT—

LOOK, THERE'S A RED INDIAN!

LET'S GO TALK TO HIM.

FORTUNATELY, THE RED INDIAN SPOKE ENGLISH—

HOW!

ER... GOOD MORNING!

YES! NICE, SUNNY MORNING ISN'T IT?

IT WON'T BE LIKE THAT IN A FEW DAYS' TIME!

WHAT DO YOU MEAN?

IT WILL RAIN HEAVILY FOR THREE DAYS AND AFTER THAT THERE WILL BE STRONG WINDS FOR TWO DAYS...

...AND THEN IT WILL BE SUNNY ONCE AGAIN.

WONDERFUL! THESE PRIMITIVE RED INDIANS KNOW MORE ABOUT THE SECRETS OF NATURE THAN WE DO.

BUT HOW DO YOU KNOW THAT?

I HEARD IT ON THE RADIO!

EH!

314

Meet the OWL

Script: Vaijayanti Wagle

Illustrations: Ajit Vasaikar

THE LAST RAYS OF THE EVENING SUN FADE AWAY. HIDDEN IN A ROCKY LEDGE ON THE OUTSKIRTS OF TOWN, THE OWL BLINKS OPEN HIS ENORMOUS EYES.

HE FLIES OUT AND SETTLES ON HIS FAVOURITE PERCH. BU BO, BU BO, HE ANNOUNCES SOLEMNLY.

A FAINT RUSTLING SOUND REACHES HIS EARS. HE TURNS HIS HEAD ALMOST RIGHT AROUND TO LOOK FOR THE SOURCE OF THE SOUND...

ISN'T IT WONDERFUL THAT HE CAN LOOK ALL AROUND HIM WITHOUT STIRRING FROM HIS PERCH?

...AND IS JUST IN TIME TO SEE A RAT RUSH INTO A THICKET.

PRESENTLY A FAINT NIBBLING SOUND REACHES HIS EARS. THE RAT IS GNAWING ON A BLADE OF GRASS.

GUIDED BY THE SOUND, THE OWL SWOOPS AS SILENTLY AS A WHISPER.

315

THE RAT DOES NOT REALISE WHAT IS HAPPENING UNTIL THE OWL'S POWERFUL CLAWS DIG INTO ITS BODY...

... AND THEN IT'S TOO LATE.

OWLS CAN CATCH PREY IN ABSOLUTE DARKNESS, RELYING ON THEIR SENSE OF HEARING ALONE.

OOPS! THE OWL HAS SWALLOWED THE RAT IN A SINGLE GULP!

WHAT HE CANNOT DIGEST, WILL BE PRESSED INTO A HARD PELLET AND PASSED OUT THROUGH HIS MOUTH.

SOME WEEKS LATER WE SEE OUR FRIEND AGAIN. THIS TIME INSTEAD OF SWOOPING ON RATS, HE IS FLYING AROUND A FEMALE OWL.

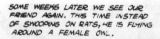

BESIDES RATS, OWLS ALSO EAT FROGS, OTHER SMALL ANIMALS, FISHES AND CRABS.

316

THEY'RE GOING TO RAISE A FAMILY...

...AND AS OWLS DON'T BUILD NESTS, THIS HOLLOW COULD BE JUST THE PLACE FOR THE FEMALE TO LAY HER EGGS IN.

SHE USUALLY LAYS FOUR CREAMY, OVAL EGGS. AND SHE SITS ON THE EGGS TO INCUBATE THEM.

FIVE WEEKS LATER THE FIRST EGG HAS HATCHED. THE OTHERS WILL FOLLOW SOON AFTER.

YOU HAVE JUST READ ABOUT THE GREAT HORNED OWL. THERE ARE MANY KINDS OF OWLS FOUND IN INDIA.

BARN OWL

COLLARED SCOPS OWL

BROWN FISH OWL

BARRED JUNGLE OWLET

THE SPOTTED OWL

317

Shikari Shambu

Script :
Luis M Fernandes
Illustrations:
V.B. Halbe

I'VE BEEN ASKED TO HUNT DOWN A DANGEROUS LEOPARD...

...A MAN-EATER!

MAKE SURE YOU'RE BACK B4 TEA-TIME!

MOTHER IS ARRIVING TODAY AND WE HAVE TO MEET HER AT THE BUS-STOP AT 5 O'CLOCK!

DOES SHE EXPECT ME TO DROP EVERYTHING AND RUSH TO THE BUS-STOP AT 5 O'CLOCK?!

ONCE WE HUNTERS ARE ON THE TRAIL OF AN ANIMAL WE LOSE ALL SENSE OF TIME!

I WON'T RETURN TILL I'VE BAGGED THAT LEOPARD!

AH, HERE'S MY MACHAN.

319

NOW I'M IN BIGGER TROUBLE... I'M HEADING STRAIGHT FOR THE WATERFALL!

EEEE-YOW!

KER-SPLOSH!

THANK HEAVENS, I'M STILL IN ONE PIECE...

FOR A MOMENT, I THOUGHT...

SO THERE YOU ARE!

WHY ARE YOU SO LATE?! GET OUT OF THAT WATER QUICKLY!

!

THE BUS IS HERE! COME ON!

SOMEHOW SHE ALWAYS GETS HER WAY.

HAVE A HAIRCUT

This story by
Dr (Mrs) Kavery Bhatt
won a Consolation Prize
in the Tinkle
Original Story Competition.

Script: Dev Nadkarni

Illustrations: V.B. Halbe

AND SO, THE BOYS GOT TO WORK IN AN UNOCCUPIED BACK ROOM OF RAFIQ'S HOUSE.

THIS IS GOING TO BE FUN!

PHEW! THIS IS HARD WORK!

WHERE DO WE GET THE MONEY TO BUY ALL THE EQUIPMENT FROM?

LET'S MAKE DO WITH WHAT WE HAVE, MANI.

RAFIQ, YOUR SISTER RAZIA COULD HELP US, PERHAPS.

HMM... I'LL GET HER SCISSORS, COMBS AND MAYBE EVEN HER SHAMPOOS AND PERFUMES. I'LL BE BACK.

AND I'LL GET A LEMON.. CURES DANDRUFF YOU KNOW— AND EGGS FOR LONGER HAIR.

GREAT! AND DON'T FORGET A MIRROR!

A FEW HOURS LATER—

THERE! WE'RE ALMOST READY.

LET'S PUT UP THE BILL-BOARD.

NOW WE'RE IN BUSINESS!

UNIQUE
Hair Dressing
SALOON

ORDINARY RS. 0-50
SPECIAL RS. 1-00
SUPER
SPECIAL RS. 2-00

NOT YET! WE MUST GET SOMEONE TO INAUGURATE IT FIRST.

WHO SHALL WE CALL?

HEY, THERE GOES MANI'S GRANDFATHER ON HIS EVENING WALK.

GOOD EVENING, GRANDPA. WE CORDIALLY INVITE YOU AS CHIEF GUEST TO INAUGURATE...

ME? AS CHIEF GUEST... TO INAUGURATE WHAT?

WE'RE STARTING A SALOON, GRANDPA— TO SERVE THE PEOPLE OF OUR COLONY...

AND WE DO BELIEVE IN DIGNITY OF LABOUR...

OKAY, OKAY, BOYS, I'LL BE HAPPY TO INAUGURATE YOUR SALOON!

DEAR, DEAR, GRANDPA.

HOW NICE!

AT THE SALOON—

GOD BLESS YOU CHILDREN, GOD BLESS YOU!

THANK YOU VERY MUCH, GRANDPA.

MY PLEASURE, BOYS...AND DO YOUR JOB WELL.

WE SHOULD START BY GIVING A FREE HAIRCUT TO A DESERVING PERSON.

I'LL GO GET SOMEBODY.

A LITTLE WHILE LATER—

WAA...WAA... BUT I DON'T WANT A HAIRCUT!

O, YOU DO— LOOK AT ALL THE JUNGLE!

IT WAS CHANDU, MANI'S 6-YEAR-OLD BROTHER.

NOW YOU JUST SIT HERE.

THERE YOU ARE, JAI, YOU CAN BEGIN.

325

326

327

328

Readers' Choice

THE FOLLY OF IMITATION

Illustrations: Ram Waeerkar

Based on a story sent by Shashin S. Kowshik, Bombay

EARLY ONE MORNING IN A VILLAGE —

?

ER... SIR, I SAW YOU GOING ROUND YOUR HOUSE SEVERAL TIMES. WHY DID YOU DO THAT?

SO THAT I'LL HAVE A GOOD HARVEST AND BECOME RICH.

SO THAT'S THE WAY TO BECOME RICH!

THE MAN WAS A ROBBER AND SO THE FOLLOWING DAY —

I'LL GO AROUND THIS HOUSE A FEW TIMES BEFORE BREAKING IN.

Make your own
SOAP BUBBLES

You will need:
Water, sugar, soap scrapings, a slim hollow plastic tube or a wire frame and a small piece of fine cloth.

Put four teaspoons of sugar into a glass.

Fill the glass with water and stir well until sugar dissolves.

Add one teaspoon of soap scrapings and stir until dissolved.

Strain the liquid into a cup through the piece of cloth.

Make a lollipop shape wire frame with old fuse or other wire.

Using the wire frame or slim plastic tube, you can blow enough bubbles to fill a room!

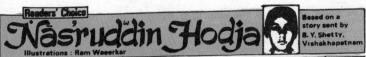

AS HODJA APPROACHED THE MEN—

WHAT WERE THEY QUARRELLING ABOUT?

THEY WERE QUARRELLING ABOUT WHO SHOULD TAKE MY BLANKET WHEN I CAME OUT TO WATCH THEM FIGHTING.

THE WISE FOOLS OF MOIRA

A folk tale from Goa

Script :
Luis M. Fernandes

Illustrations:
Ram Waeerkar

THE CATHOLIC VILLAGERS OF MOIRA HAD LONG FELT THAT THEIR CHURCH WAS NOT BIG ENOUGH TO HOLD THE LARGE CONGREGATION. ONE DAY THEY HELD A MEETING TO DECIDE HOW TO REMEDY THE SITUATION.

LET'S BUILD AN EXTENSION.

AN EXTENSION WOULD LOOK VERY UGLY.

LET'S BREAK DOWN THE WHOLE STRUCTURE AND BUILD A NEW CHURCH.

IT WOULD REQUIRE A LOT OF MONEY TO BREAK DOWN THE CHURCH AND BUILD A NEW ONE.

WHY BREAK IT DOWN AT ALL?

WHEN A COCONUT OR MANGO TREE IS STUNTED, WHAT DO WE DO?

WE LOOSEN THE SOIL AT THE BASE, DIG IT UP...

...AND LAY MANURE.

EXACTLY.

337

339

SO IF WE WANT TO BRING THE CHURCH FORWARD...

...WE SHOULD GO BEHIND THE CHURCH AND PUSH IT!

WHAT A SIMPLE SOLUTION!

ISN'T IT?

LET'S DO IT AT ONCE!

YES.

I'LL CALL ALL THE MEN TOGETHER.

YES, DO THAT.

SOON ALL THE ABLE-BODIED MEN OF THE VILLAGE HAD ASSEMBLED BEHIND THE CHURCH.

SHALL WE START PUSHING?

NOT YET.

IT WOULD BE EASIER TO PUSH THE CHURCH IF SOMETHING SMOOTH WAS PLACED UNDER IT.

LET'S SPREAD WOOLLEN BLANKETS IN FRONT OF THE CHURCH RIGHT UP TO THE SPOT WHERE WE WANT IT TO BE PUSHED.

AN EXCELLENT IDEA.

THE VILLAGERS GATHERED A LARGE PILE OF WOOLLEN BLANKETS AND SPREAD THEM IN FRONT OF THE CHURCH.

340

341

...AND KEPT THEM THERE.

THEN HE RAN OUT AGAIN, AND AFTER SOME TIME —

STOP! STOP!

IT'S REACHED THE LIMIT!

THE VILLAGERS RAN TO THE FRONT OF THE CHURCH.

SEE, ALL THE BLANKETS HAVE GONE UNDER.

THEY HAVE INDEED!

WE'VE DONE IT! WE'VE PUSHED THE CHURCH FORWARD!

THERE WAS GREAT REJOICING IN THE VILLAGE THAT DAY AND THE SACRISTAN WAS PRAISED TO THE SKIES.

Write a Letter with Your Own Invisible Ink

You will need: a lime; an old fountain pen; a cup; a sheet of white paper; a source of heat (a candle).

Squeeze the lime and collect its juice in the cup

Dip the old pen into the juice and write out a 'secret' letter on the piece of paper. After you have written 4-5 words, dip the pen again into the juice. You cannot read what you have written. Your letter is an invisible one.

To be able to read it, hold the letter close to a candle for a minute or so. The words will appear slowly in a brownish colour.

TINKLE is an ideal magazine for younger children.

(N.B. Do not hold this letter too close to the candle, for it may catch fire.)

THE STUPID THIEF

Illustrations: Ram Waeerkar

Based on a story sent by
Snigdhá Bose, Cuttack

BUDDHURAM WAS PASSING THROUGH A FOREST ONE DAY WHEN—

ROBBERS!

SO MUCH LOOT!

HE QUIETLY SLIPPED AWAY.

HUH! THIS IS LIFE! WHY TOIL AND SWEAT? I'LL ALSO BECOME A THIEF!

SO THE NEXT NIGHT, ARMED WITH A KNIFE AND A SACK, BUDDHURAM SET OUT.

THERE MUST BE PLENTY OF MONEY IN THAT HOUSE.

HE WENT ROUND THE HOUSE.

AHA! I'M IN LUCK! THIS IS OPEN!

THUD!

WHO IS THAT?

344

345

346

JACKALS CAME TO DINNER

Illustrations: Ashok Dongre

Based on a story sent by Rajesh Kumar Prasad, Assam

AN OLD WOMAN WAS TAKING FOOD FOR HER SON WHO WORKED IN THE FIELDS.

SUDDENLY—

JACKALS!

WHAT HAVE YOU GOT THERE, GRANDMA?

S- SOME KHICHARI FOR MY SON.

PUT IT DOWN! NOW COME AND PRESS OUR LEGS.

WHILE SHE PRESSED THE LEGS OF ONE JACKAL, THE OTHERS ATE UP ALL THE KHICHARI!

THE OLD WOMAN RETURNED HOME BADLY—

MY POOR BOY MUST BE VERY HUNGRY.

THAT EVENING WHEN HER SON RETURNED—

WHAT HAPPENED? WHY DIDN'T YOU BRING MY LUNCH TODAY?

I...I HAD A STRANGE EXPERIENCE...

AND SHE TOLD HER SON WHAT HAD HAPPENED.

...I COULDN'T GET FOOD THROUGH TO YOU BECAUSE OF THE JACKALS.

THE JACKALS CONTINUED TO HARASS THE OLD WOMAN, UNTIL ONE EVENING—

LISTEN, MOTHER, I HAVE A PLAN...

SO THE NEXT DAY THE OLD WOMAN WENT TO THE FOREST AND BEGAN TO PICK FLOWERS.

?!

WHY IS THERE NO KHICHARI TODAY?

MY SON IS DEAD. SO FOR WHOM SHOULD I BRING THE KHICHARI?

BUT I WOULD LIKE TO COOK FOR SOMEONE. WHY DON'T YOU ALL COME AND HAVE DINNER WITH ME TOMORROW?

348

THE NEXT EVENING THE JACKALS WENT TO THE OLD WOMAN'S HOUSE.

SHE WENT INTO THE KITCHEN AND STARTED SPRINKLING WATER ON A HOT GRIDDLE.

SIZZLE

SHE MUST BE MAKING PURIS.

OR KACHORIS!

IS THE FOOD READY?

YES. BUT I DON'T WANT YOU ALL TO FIGHT FOR THE FOOD AS YOU USUALLY DO...

...SO I WILL TIE YOU UP, FIRST.

DO IT QUICKLY THEN! WE'RE STARVING.

THE OLD WOMAN TIED UP THE JACKALS...

...AND THEN —

SON! SON! COME WITH THE IRON ROD!

SON?

349